THE FEDERATION PROTECTS

CONNOR WHITELEY

No part of this book may be reproduced in any form or by any electronic or mechanical means. Including information storage, and retrieval systems, without written permission from the author except for the use of brief quotations in a book review.

This book is NOT legal, professional, medical, financial or any type of official advice.

Any questions about the book, rights licensing, or to contact the author, please email connorwhiteley@connorwhiteley.net

Copyright © 2023 CONNOR WHITELEY

All rights reserved.

DEDICATION
Thank you to all my readers without you I couldn't do what I love.

CHAPTER 1
4th August 2022
London, England

Private Eye Bettie English flat out loved Private Eye Con.

It might have officially been known as the British Private Eye Federation, Private Eye Con was a far, far better name for such an amazing convention, because unlike other professional organisations who ran long boring conferences.

The Federation did not.

Bettie loved how much fun each convention was with its laughter, thrilling line up of speakers and there were always rumours and conversations to have with different people, and that was why Bettie came to these conventions.

Sure it was great to hear about the latest investigative techniques from time to time, but Bettie had been doing this long enough to know what worked, and what seriously didn't work. So each year she came to Private Eye Con to learn the rumours, the going-ons and anything else she could from her fellow Private Eyes.

And this year was no different.

As Bettie sat on a wonderfully soft wooden chair at a small wooden table with three other chairs neatly tucked in, she had her hand firmly around a small ornate glass of orange juice like it was the most expensive whiskey in the world.

Bettie had never been a fan of whiskey but she couldn't drink for at least another month with her twins coming. And whilst she had gotten more than enough funny looks from the convention staff, she still wanted to be here.

And it wasn't actually like she had much of a choice, the Federation President David Osborne (A great friend of Bettie) would probably never forgive her for not turning up, especially as she had stupidly agreed to speak on some panels.

Even now she didn't know why she agreed to it, but she had a feeling it had something to do with her inability to say no to David. He was such a great kind leader who seriously protected all Private Eyes, no matter their sex, sexuality or race.

The wonderful sound of distant laughing, people rolling around the last few display units and the pouring of drinks made Bettie really pleased to be back in the convention environment. And the best freshly delivered fish and chips made Bettie's mouth water.

She loved the crispy golden batter of the fish and the crunchiness of the perfectly seasoned chips.

There was just one problem.

Bettie couldn't eat anything that came from an animal since she got pregnant. She had tried and tried and tried, but her body flat out disagreed with all of it. Thankfully with vegan food coming along in such leaps and bounds over the years Bettie was able to eat like most people.

Including vegan fish and chips and Bettie was seriously looking forward to that.

With the sensational smell of the fish and chips getting closer and closer, Bettie had to swallow a few times to stop her mouth was salivating too much. And this was what she really enjoyed about being on the Prep-crew for the convention, she loved her fellow organisers.

Private Eye Con was a three day event that happened every single August without fail, and it had always been like that since its founding in the darkest days of The Great War, so it ran Friday morning to Sunday afternoon. Giving people plenty of time to catch the train home.

But those in the know never did that, because there were some legendary after-parties once the Convention closed. And some of the organisers had promised Bettie some no-alcohol after parties if she wanted to attend.

Bettie had all but confirmed she was going, but she loved how all the Private Eyes respected, love and admired her. She didn't know a single other profession where people would bend over backwards to make a party for a pregnant woman.

Not a single one.

Bettie took a sip of freshly squeezed orange juice and the pure refreshing flavour exploded in her mouth, and she loved it.

"Bettie!" a man shouted, clearly pleased to see her.

Bettie looked past the rows upon rows of other wooden tables towards the massive ornate wooden doors to see three people walking with steaming hot bags of fish and chips.

Bettie recognised them instantly as some truly amazing people and she had worked with them for most of the day finishing up the preparations for the convention.

The two in front of the little group were two middle-aged men with massive smiles on their faces, and they were twin brothers. Logan and Leo Natt.

Bettie had always liked Logan with his white shirt, stylish jeans and kind looking face. Everyone in the Federation knew him as the best Private Eye in the country if you needed anything done so delicately the clients couldn't risk having the police involved.

"Bet," Leo said, as he started to dish up the fish and chips.

Bettie also had a lot of time for Leo, he wasn't as good as his brother as a Private Eye but he tried, and he was always helpful at the Federation's events, so everyone sort of tolerated him.

But Bettie had to admit he had been utterly useless earlier trying to make a display stand together. It really wasn't that hard. Bettie had ended up having to wobble over, click two things together and sort it out for him.

When everyone sat down, Bettie smiled at the woman who sat opposite her. Ivy Collins was an amazing woman, she was actually the first female Private Eye to be allowed into the Federation towards the end of the 60s. She had fought to prove herself then and ever since.

Bettie was really impressed that even though she was now close to 90, Ivy was still fighting fit and helping out as much as she could. But there was another reason why Bettie loved seeing Ivy. Because Ivy always knew exactly what was going on before anyone else did.

"When's David coming?" Bettie asked.

Ivy picked up her fork and stabbed her fish a few times.

"David's coming tomorrow morning. Apparently he's bringing a special guest for the Convention, he's been sorting them out," Ivy said.

"Come on Iv, you must know who it is," Leo said.

Ivy smiled. "I actually don't, but there are two things I wanted to announce to you all, as some of my closest friends,"

Bettie took a bite of the amazingly golden crispy

vegan fish. It was amazing.

"I want you all to be the first to know I'm properly retiring on Sunday from the Private Eye world," Ivy said.

Bettie coughed. She almost choked on her fish.

"Why!" Bettie asked louder than she wanted to.

"I'll be ninety next week pet," Ivy said, "I've had an amazing career, but I want to enjoy the rest of my days with my husband in Cornwall. So I will no longer be Secretary General of the Federation,"

Bettie slowly nodded. She didn't like it, when Bettie had first become a member, it had been Ivy that taught her the tricks of Federation politics, who to avoid and how to survive the sexist elements that still lived inside the organisation.

And even now Ivy was like a best friend or mother-figure to Bettie, it was going to be a hell of a loss to the Private Eye world.

Bettie raised her glass of orange juice. "I wish you the best of luck,"

Everyone else raised their glasses, and Ivy blew everyone a kiss.

"Thank you loves," Ivy said.

"What's the other thing?" Logan asked.

Ivy gave him an evil smile. "I was given permission from David to tell you something. But no one else can know until the Opening Ceremony tomorrow. Do you all understand?"

Everyone nodded. Bettie felt her babies kick almost as if they were excited about the news, Bettie wasn't excited. This concerned her.

"At the Opening Ceremony tomorrow, David will announce he is retiring from the Federation,"

"No!" Bettie shouted.

Leo and Logan looked equally shocked.

David was actually one of the most important people in the entire Federation, and he was definitely the greatest leader in their history. Bettie had always liked him, and compared to some of the other senior Private Eyes, he actually valued the opinions of women, people of colour and people who weren't born in England.

And maybe the most important (and Bettie's favourite thing about him) was every single person in the Federation respected him. No matter their sex, race or political orientation, they respected him right out.

That had really become clear in recent years with the political tensions around the UK political parties, Brexit and everything else happening in the UK. Bettie had been pretty sure the Federation might split twice in the past few years, but it was David who had managed to hold it together.

Making the Federation stronger in the process.

Bettie had no idea who would take over, but whoever it was would have some immense shoes to fill. She almost felt sorry for that person.

"Who's going to take over?" Logan asked.

Ivy finished off her chips. "It's up to David to decide. He hasn't revealed anything to me Pet, but it wouldn't be you. I can promise you that,"

Bettie smiled. She was definitely pleased about that.

"He will reveal who is his successor on Sunday at the closing ceremony Pet. The entire weekend will be overshadowed by it for sure, but David wants to see how everyone reacts to the chaos and excitement the announcement causes,"

Bettie nodded. Whatever happened this weekend, one thing was clear.

It was going to be extremely interesting.

And extremely chaotic.

The most two powerful positions in the Federation were open.

Bettie knew that only meant one thing.

Utter chaos.

And chaos breeds danger.

CHAPTER 2
5th August 2022
London, England

Detective Graham Adams couldn't actually remember how long he had been with his beautiful sexy girlfriend Bettie, but he absolutely knew it was at least two years. And neither of the past two years had persuaded him to go to Private Eye Con, as far as he was concerned it was filled with wannabe Private Eyes and failed police officers.

Graham still wasn't sure about attending the convention, seeing all the Private Eyes and learning all the illegal things that they did. But with Bettie a month away from giving birth, he wanted to be close by just in case, and to his utter horror Bettie had really jumped at the chance for him to attend.

Even now that still terrified Graham because his worst nightmare would be being forced to be on some kind of panel about how Private Eyes could be better. He would flat out hate that.

As Graham stepped out the massive golden revolving doors into the lobby of Hotel Grandeur, his mouth actually dropped. Sure Graham had heard of how grand this hotel in particular was, and it was where all the major London conventions happened that weren't big enough to attract media attention.

But Graham had not expected this.

The lobby might have only been the size of an Olympic swimming pool or two, but its walls were covered in solid gold, rubies and expensive artwork hung elegantly on the walls. Graham was just amazed, he had never seen such beauty in all his life, he was actually wondered how much it was worth.

The glimmering sunlight reflecting off the smooth oak desk made Graham focus dead ahead to see so many men in tight business suits and women in wonderful dresses. There were tons of people here getting checked into the hotel.

From what Graham had seen online, the Hotel Grandeur had two thousand hotel rooms, four presidential suites and the convention chamber was a kilometre long and half a kilometre wide.

He still couldn't understand why Bettie had complained that it was a tat too small for everything they wanted to do.

And amazingly enough the lobby actually had a slight chill in the air, but it was a very nice chill. Graham had expected the lobby to be boiling hot and awful with all these people checking in, but no. It was just the right temperature, and considering how boiling hot it was outside, Graham loved the coolness of the lobby.

This was going to be a great weekend.

The entire lobby smelt of jasmine, raspberries and lemon that somehow worked together to create a seriously welcoming and almost seductive smell into the hotel.

And it made the taste of raspberry and lemon cheesecake form on his tongue. Graham really missed the ones his grandmother used to make for him as a kid.

Graham looked around to see if there was a queue or something, but nope, all the Private Eyes were assembled en-mass in some kind of organisation. But the hotel staff seemed to be dealing with people quickly enough.

As much as Graham wanted to see Bettie and kiss and hug her, he was a bit disappointed she'd texted him and told him she had to finish up her notes for the first panel. Something about *Being A Woman Private Eye In A Men's World*.

Graham really wanted to be there for that talk, not only because he wanted Bettie to see a friendly face (even though she probably knew every single person attending by first name), but because he wanted to understand what she faced at conventions like this.

Especially as he never liked to mention how grumpy she was for the first few hours she returned home after each year's convention.

"Graham!" someone said.

Graham had no clue who would know him who was here. He only knew Bettie and the Federation President, everyone else here was a mystery.

Graham turned around and smiled when he saw Bettie's nephew Sean walk in with his suitcase wearing his tight black jeans, white shirt and with his longish blond hair with very stylish pink highlights running through it.

"Where's Auntie?" Sean asked.

"Sorting out some stuff for her panel. Bet didn't tell me you were coming," Graham said.

"She didn't tell any of us," another woman said.

Graham laughed a little when a tall woman stepped out from behind Sean wearing a very formal dress, diamond necklace and black high heels. Graham was really surprised to see Bettie's sister Phryne here.

Graham wanted to say something but his mouth didn't allow any words to come out.

"We're just as surprised as you are," Phryne said, clearly not impressed at being summoned.

"What did she say to you?" Graham asked Sean.

"She wanted me to come for support and she's thought I'll like it," Sean said. "Then I found out mum was invited too,"

Phryne frowned. "I had a very important legal meeting with my firm today, then I get a call from my boss saying him and the President wanted my attendance at this god awful place,"

Graham wasn't exactly sure him and Phryne were seeing the same place. The hotel was stunning.

"You know Bettie isn't President right?" Sean asked.

Phryne huffed. "Well now I do!"

Graham smiled at Sean. This was going to be interesting with Phryne to say the least.

"Where do we even get registered or whatever these people do?" Phryne asked.

"You must be Phryne," a man said behind Graham.

Graham looked around and saw a very tall young man in a tight silk blue suit walk towards them. Graham wondered if Sean's eyes were about to pop out of his head.

"Sean, where's your boyfriend Harry?" Graham asked, smiling.

Sean playfully hit Graham. "He's at an intense therapy centre this week,"

Graham nodded. For that moment he had sadly forgotten about Harry's brain injuries and all the therapy he was having just to help him, the only possible comfort of the entire thing was the doctors were certain Harry would make a full recovery within another 18 months.

Graham really hoped he would.

The young man bowed slightly to Phryne as he hooked his arm inside her.

"Your sister didn't tell me how stunning you looked," he said.

Phryne frowned. "Listen to me idiot. I don't play men's games. Why am I here?"

Graham simply stood next to Sean. If something was going to go down, he wanted a front row seat.

"The President of the Federation wants your legal opinion on something, and your firm agreed to be a sponsor of the convention if we officially recommend your firm to our guests,"

Graham had never seen someone change as much as Phryne did. Her entire face lit up like a Christmas tree, her voice became velvety soft and she seriously played into the young man's seductive act.

Then the two of them simply walked off together.

Graham just looked at Sean and smiled. "How badly do you want to be your mum right now?"

Sean smiled and shook his head. "Tell me how badly you want to check-in,"

Graham wasn't sure what he meant so he looked through the mass of people towards the front desk, and wow... Sean was definitely right. Graham had never seen such a stunning blond woman in his entire life.

Graham simply looked away. "Looking is never a bad thing. Acting is when it becomes bad,"

"Nice save," Bettie said behind Graham.

Graham turned around and laughed. He really missed not seeing Bettie and they might not have been each other for 24 hours, but it really had felt like a lifetime for Graham.

He kissed her. Hard. Repeatedly.

Bettie shook her head with a smile, and then hugged Sean.

"Here are your hotel passes and keys," Bettie said giving Graham and Sean a white key card, a leaflet and a goody bag.

Graham looked inside and he had no idea why the goody bag contained fingerprint powder, two chocolate bars and a bunch of utter crap given to the Federation probably from sponsors.

Bettie kissed Graham. "I need to see David before the Opening Ceremony. You'll be at my panel?"

Graham truly smiled at her. "Wouldn't miss it for the world,"

Bettie gave him a final kiss, Sean a hug and then she disappeared into the crowd.

And now he was finally here, Graham was rather looking forward to it.

If only for the fact he got to spend it with the woman he loved.

And hopefully not solve a single crime.

But he seriously doubted it.

CHAPTER 3
5th August 2022
London, England

It had been great to see Sean and Graham earlier and as weird as it sounded, Bettie really had missed Graham for the past day. It still felt so weird to her because she had had past boyfriends before, and she never ever felt like this with any of them.

And that's including one of the relationships that lasted for five years, but Bettie really loved Graham, and thankfully he really, really loved her.

As Bettie sat on a very comfortable black fabric chair on the central stage (which was a very elegant wooden platform) in the middle of the conference chamber. Bettie felt so special and important and privileged to be sitting here.

There were three other chairs next to Bettie's, and she was really glad to have Ivy, Leon and Logan sitting on the stage just in case they were needed to support David in his speech.

Bettie had already given her opening address to the Convention about how great it was to see everyone again, and she quickly introduced herself, Ivy and the Natt twins.

Granted Bettie didn't know a few people here, but as she was standing on the stage talking, it was amazing to feel like she was with family again. Because that's what Private Eyes were to each other.

Some strange dysfunctional family.

From Bettie's seat, she could see all the hundreds and hundreds of little stalls, tables and mini-stages that lined up and down the kilometre long conference chamber, and she was surprised it was so packed.

There had to easily be two thousand people here, the vast majority of them were members and then the rest were either so-called special guests and the rest were probably wannabe Private Eyes.

The entire convention chamber smelt so crispy and refreshing with its hints of pine, lavender and cream cakes that made the most sensational taste of freshly baked sponges form on her tongue. But the chamber probably had until tonight for the smell to change.

From all Bettie's experience at these conventions, it only took one day for these conventions to start smelling of sweat, smoke and other less pleasant smells. Especially as some Private Eyes didn't like to wash as much as they should.

Bettie always made a point to avoid those people.

The sound of President Davis Obsorne's

booming, authoritative and wonderful voice filled the entire space as Bettie looked at the sea of faces staring at him. And every single face was smiling at him like he was some kind of divine prophet delivering such wisdom.

And in a way he actually was, Bettie loved listening to David speak. There was always such wisdom to his words, and he could somehow make the most boring topic sound utterly fascinating.

Bettie supposed it was because of his age, his diplomatic skills and how smart he looked in his grey suit, waistcoat and expensive silk shirt.

"... so I shall retire at the end of the convention and per Federation Rules, I will name my successor. Therefore, I shall declare this Private Eye Con officially open!" David said.

Bettie just placed her hands on her baby bump as she actually heard the words. It was one thing to know it was going to happen, but very much a completely different thing to actually hear it and have it confirmed.

Judging by the gasps, screams and moans in the audience, everyone else agreed to. It didn't seem real.

Then to Bettie's disappointment, everyone started to break out in little groups of conversations and started to walk away. From what Bettie could understand they were all talking about who could be the next leader, what chaos would happen now and most important would the Federation split.

It was that last comment Bettie didn't fully

understand. Sure she understood with all the political upheaval in the UK at the moment everything and everyone was getting very polarised politically, but it was a stupid idea to imagine it would cause the Federation to split.

David started to walk over to Bettie and the three other organisers. Bettie stood up and gave David a quick hug.

"So it's official then," Bettie said.

David frowned. "I... I'm sorry I didn't tell *you*. It was too hard,"

"So you had me tell her," Ivy said.

David shrugged. "I better not keep you from your panels. Natt twins, sorry but I had to change your panel location to the very back of the chamber,"

Bettie wasn't sure why the Natt twins looked so happy about that. It was a well known rule at the convention that the panels at the very back were never good, and the only people that turned up were the wannabes that believed all the myths.

Bettie didn't want to see, hear or feel all the abuse they would give the Natt twins for telling them that Private Eye work was mostly background checks.

Wannabes seriously hated being told that!

Ivy tapped Bettie's arm three times. "I better go two Pet, I'll get my notebook and a coffee and be back here in five,"

Bettie nodded. She was really looking forward to being on a panel with Ivy and some of the other top female Private Eyes.

David gently took Bettie's shoulder and guided her around so they could talk without many people being able to see what he was saying.

Bettie knew that was a wise move considering a good number of Private Eyes could read lips.

"Bettie, how... how would you advise me on picking a successor?" David asked.

Bettie cocked her head. "Dave, you're a great man. You must have some idea who to give your title and position to,"

David just looked at her.

"You know the different elements wouldn't have a woman as President," Bettie said.

David laughed. "You better not say that on your panel,"

Bettie smiled and rolled her eyes.

"Fine Bet," David said, "I will decide on someone. Who wouldn't you like to see President?"

Bettie opened her mouth, but she didn't feel comfortable just saying a name, and she wanted to be a bit kind anyway.

"Personally I wouldn't follow anyone from the more extreme elements of the Federation. No far-right, far-left and no hate elements,"

David smiled. "You always were the diplomatic one of us. I already wasn't going to pick them, I'll let you crack on my dear. I'll see you tonight at dinner. The Federation Protects,"

"The Federation Protects," Bettie said as David walked away.

Bettie was never too sure where that particular saying had come from but she liked it. Partly because it made her feel like she was part of some kind of cult's inner circle and she had power.

But she also liked it because it was true. The Federation truly protected its members, and that made Bettie even more concerned about the convention.

She had known David for decades and he had always made up his mind before he made a decision, sure he almost always ran a decision by herself or Ivy first. But this time felt different.

It felt like David had created a storm without knowing its direction. And that concerned Bettie.

Private Eyes were a dangerous lot. Private Eyes knew how to solve and commit crimes.

Bettie just didn't know if anyone would cross that line to become president.

But anything was possible.

And that's what scared Bettie.

CHAPTER 4
5th August 2022
London, England

Graham had always (without fail) considered himself to be an understanding man, and whilst far from every single cop in the police force bothered with trying to understand others. Graham really tried to. Because he fully believed that if the police don't bother to understand the people they're *meant* to serve and protect, then how were they ever meant to improve relationships with the public.

So if there was ever a talk for police officers from gay, black or any other minority group, Graham made sure to be there.

But this talk on Being A Woman Private Eye In A Man's World was something else, Graham had expected a few stories about sexism and everything else, but not some of the things said. Like sexual harassment, extreme bullying and outright assault.

As Graham sat on a hard plastic chair at the very

back of the audience which was made of mostly of women, but Graham couldn't tell if they were wannabe or real Private Eyes, and Graham just focused on his stunning girlfriend as Bettie stood on the main stage taking complete control.

Graham had to admit he had seen Bettie do tons of great work over the years, so she was an amazing speaker. She somehow managed to captivate the audience as she moved about the stage, managing the questions, the panellists and keep it all rather fascinating.

Since in Graham's experience that was the harsh truth about speakers on this topic, some feminist speakers were so caught up in their speeches that it sounded more like a "all men must die" type of talk, then on the other side, you had speakers who were so boring in their talks everyone switched off.

Graham felt sorry for those speakers, because he truly believed all women, men and minority groups should be equal. But sometimes telling others that was an impossible task, and somehow his amazing girlfriend was managing it.

Perfectly.

Graham almost gagged as the man sitting to his right stunk of body odour, sweat and his own urine. He smelt so disgusting that Graham wondered when he last showered.

But it was great to see Sean sitting to Graham's left, nodding along almost like he had experienced most of the same hate the speakers had. Graham still hated when Harry and Sean had been beaten up, hospitalised and then forgotten about by the police.

Graham was more than glad those police officers had been arrested for the attack.

"Thank you Ivy," Bettie said, "so everyone that concludes the more scripted element of the panel. Questions?"

Graham smiled at Bettie as she was clearly surprised at how many hands shot up from women and men alike.

"You there," Bettie said pointing to the smelly man sitting next to Graham.

The man stood up and Graham feared he was going to pass out.

"Why you lying!" the man shouted.

Bettie cocked her head. "Sir, I can assure you everything we'd said is true,"

"Liars. This is not the truth. Women are free in the world and yet you women keep banging on about your oppression. It ends now!"

Graham felt himself tense. He prepared himself to strike. He wasn't letting this idiot do anything.

"It is women like you that keep men under their shoes. But we resist your oppression, men will be free once more!"

Graham stood up. "Leave,"

The man laughed. "You like being a slave,"

Graham pointed towards the exit. "Leave!"

Graham quickly looked at Bettie and he noticed she was holding a tiny key fob.

The man swung at Graham.

Graham ducked.

Sean jumped up.

Whacking the man.

The man fell to the ground.

A few moments later two very muscular security officers dressed in all black walked over, grabbed the man and dragged him outside.

Graham looked at Bettie to make sure she was okay, and she wasn't shaken by the entire thing.

But she looked perfectly fine like it had never happened.

"You there," Bettie said pointing to a young woman near the front.

Graham just looked at Bettie as she smiled, nodded and make everyone feel like they were all perfectly safe and nothing bad was ever going to happen to them.

Graham really needed Bettie to teach him that trick, that took some amazing skills. And Graham really loved her for that.

"Listen to the people in front," Sean said very quietly.

Graham nodded and leant slightly closer to the two women sitting in front of Sean.

"We need to get rid of competition," the older woman said.

"Yea but how. We cannot end 'em. What about this Bettie woman. Is she a threat?" the other woman asked.

"I don't know. I think we should monitor her and her interactions with the President,"

"Yea know other peeps will be scheming to,"

Graham hated the sound of that. First that sexist guy, now these two women scheming against Bettie, Graham didn't want to know what would happen next.

"Listen Doris," the older woman said, "all we need to do is be the last people standing. I know Johnny is planning some stuff to discredit the far-left. Joanna is planning the same for the far-right. Let's those groups kill each other, then we'll deal with the others,"

Doris nodded. "Still think this Bet's a problem,"

The older woman turned around and frowned at Graham.

"Do you mind? This is a private conversation,"

Sean frowned. "If you do anything to hurt my auntie, you will answer to me,"

The older woman smiled. "Believe me you little pouf, I'm not scared like a fairy boy like you,"

Graham really wanted to kick her out but the two women simply got up and left. All whilst Bettie was artfully answering questions, keeping everyone on the edge of their seats and prompting the other panellists to answer the questions to.

But with everyone scheming against each other, Graham was really glad he was here.

He didn't want Bettie to be alone right now.

Maybe him and Sean would stay real close to

Bettie.

Because he knew, just knew that something was about to happen.

And Graham couldn't live with himself if anything happened to the love of his life.

CHAPTER 5
5th August 2022
London, England

Bettie had absolutely loved today. She had been on three amazing panels, the first Being A Women Private Eye one was just brilliant. Bettie had actually forgotten how great it was chairing a panel, talking with amazing women and helping people understand the sexism they still faced.

Then the second one was one on investigative techniques, which really wasn't Bettie's favourite topic but with the original chairmen falling ill, Bettie had to take over. She had a blast.

Bettie had taken one long look at the programme for the panel, and she literally threw it away. Then her and the panellists had given such a fascinating talk Bettie did a rough count at the end and over five hundred people were listening to them.

Bettie loved that!

Then the very last talk that Bettie had to survive

hungry babies kicking inside her was on the business side of being a Private Eye, like was it a good idea to set up a legal company, how to protect your hard-earned money against being taxed and all the different types of tips and tricks that Bettie and all other long-term professionals knew.

It had been an amazing day.

As Bettie sat at a large round wooden table, she was rather surprised at how all out David and the other organisers had gone for the first official dinner of the convention. Now 8 o'clock at night might have seemed like a very late time for dinner, and it was.

But in Bettie's experience, Private Eyes always liked pre-dinner drinks, a chance to clear up after a busy day of listening to panels, talking to people at stalls and catching up with old friends, so it only made sense for dinner to be a bit later.

Bettie ran her fingers gently over the smooth silk tablecloths, linen napkins and the silver cutlery that was ever-so neatly laid out on the table for her to enjoy.

She had called Graham and Sean earlier to see if they were joining her for dinner, both had said yes, but Bettie wasn't sure where they were now. She knew Sean wanted to phone Harry for a little while to see how today's therapy sessions went, and Bettie really wanted him to tell her later.

Graham was a mystery though.

The deafening sound of people talking, laughing and commenting on all the amazing panels filled the entire dining room as everyone sat in their little groups and enjoying their starters.

The entire room smelt utterly amazing with hints of the most golden, crispy chicken goujons Bettie had ever smelt, and by the looks of the juicy succulent lamb that the waiters were walking about with, Bettie knew she was in for a treat tonight.

"Sorry we're late," Graham said as he kissed Bettie on the cheek and sat down next to her.

Sean hugged Bettie and sat down opposite her.

Bettie's mouth dropped a little as she stared at Graham in his absolutely stunning suit with his well-fitted trousers, white shirt and black blazer. He looked like the top of a wedding cake, a very sexy wedding cake.

After a few moments Bettie forced some words out.

"Where were you?" Bettie asked.

Graham frowned. "Just wanted to check with security that that idiot who called you a liar was gone,"

Bettie smiled. "Yea, he isn't the best Private Eye around,"

"You know him Auntie?"

"Yep," Bettie said, "his name is Archie William, a member of the far-far-right element within the Federation. They believe that only straight, white rich men should be allowed in the Federation,"

Sean and Graham laughed. Bettie wanted to, but with all the chaos going on in the Federation at the moment, it just didn't seem right to think anything was impossible at the moment.

"That reminds me," Graham said leaning closer. "Watch your back. I-"

Bettie waved him silent. "I know. I've overheard three groups of people making threats against me today,"

Sean looked around and presumably eyed a waiter or someone as he waved them over.

"But why would people attack you?" Sean asked. "How does this whole President thing work?"

Bettie really didn't want people to attack her, but she knew what some Private Eyes were like. Some were very dark people.

"All it is, is a President names a successor and then the new President serves as long as they want until they retire," Bettie said.

"What if the members don't like them?" Sean asked.

"Then the membership of the Federation can call a Vote Of No Confidence and then if a leader fails that. Then a new leader is democratically elected, but the Federation's been about since 1916. That's never happened,"

A very short waitress walked over holding a little notebook.

"Hello Sirs and Madam, what may I get you?" she said.

"Can I have a diet cola, BBQ ribs and a side of sweet potato chips please?" Sean asked.

"Of course sir," the waitress said.

Then Bettie and Graham ordered theirs and the waitress hurried away quickly. Bettie was really looking forward to her vegan BBQ ribs, they were amazing.

"How did the Federation get formed?" Graham asked.

Bettie smiled. She loved telling this story.

"So in World War 1 around 1916 the UK government had a massive problem. The war was going terribly bad and their spies were being picked off one by one, because back in the day it was really easy to detect spies if you were specially trained,"

"Because spies were all white, middle-class men," Sean said.

Bettie nodded. "So the Liberal Government of the time came up with the strangest idea in political history. The liberals contacted every single Private Eye in the British Empire, recruited them as spies and slowly won the war,"

"How did the Federation get formed though?" Sean asked.

"When the Liberals recruited the Private Eyes, they couldn't have their own government and security services knowing what was happening, so they formed a very secret organisation known as the Federation to manage the Private Eyes as they worked in Germany, Italian and in the Austro-Hungarian Empire,"

Bettie loved seeing Sean's and Graham's face lit

up, and that was one of the reasons why she loved the Federation. Because it had such a fascinating history.

Sean lent closer. "But I heard the Federation has powers to create UK law. I thought only the House of Lords and Parliament could create laws,"

Bettie really smiled at that. "Well at the end of the war, the Liberals and King George the 5th met with the Federation and decided to reward them for their actions so the Government passed the very first Private Eye Act,"

Bettie smiled at the waitress as she gave everyone their drinks.

"And in that Act, there is a little section dictating that Federation can create laws automatically that affect Private Eyes, their rights and anything to do with them within reason. Yet it is of course subject to Parliamentary approval,"

Someone started to tap on their glass.

Bettie looked around and smiled as she saw David stand up at the table next to them and raise his glass.

He took a sip of his red wine.

"Thank you for attending the first official dinner of the convention. I'll be quick but I want to say that tomorrow night at the Award Ceremony and General Annual Meeting of the Federation, I will be asking you all the vote on a critical matter,"

Bettie cocked her head. This was brand new to her, David hadn't mentioned any of this to her, and judging by Ivy's face next to David, she didn't know either.

David took another sip of the wine.

"When you get back to your rooms, you will find a packet detailing out a new law change I want to make to the Private Eye Act 2015, and I want your support in it before I put it towards Parliament,"

Bettie was interested. She had never heard him speak like this before.

"I want being a Private Eye to become a protected title, meaning everyone will have to be a member of the Federation and trained and licensed by us to call themselves a Private Eye," David said.

Tons of people started moaning and groaning and complaining to themselves.

David took another sip of the wine.

Bettie looked at him.

David started coughing.

Choking.

Vomiting.

Bettie shot up.

The crimes had begun.

CHAPTER 6
5th August 2022
London, England

Graham saw David Osborne collapse with his hand round his own throat, Graham wasn't letting anything happen to the President.

Graham and Bettie rushed over.

Graham grabbed David and started slapping him on the back whilst Bettie loosen David's tie.

He kept vomiting.

Graham tilted his head forward so David wouldn't choke on his own vomit. Then Graham helped him onto the ground and put him in the recovery position so there was no way he could roll onto his back and choke on his sick.

When Graham stood up he saw Bettie, Sean and Ivy were the only people calling for an ambulance, and Graham just stared at everyone else who was standing around their large wooden tables having dinner.

No one did anything.

Now Graham could easily understand people not reacting in a normal situation, because the vast majority of people weren't freezers in an emergency, and Graham appreciated that not everyone liked to run towards danger.

But he equally expected some people to be call-for-helpers, yet the only people doing that were the only three people Graham knew for sure were runners-towards-danger.

So it begged the question, why did everyone hesitate or not bother to help the only man who could make them President?

It made no sense whatsoever.

Graham looked at Bettie as she came over to him and he smiled a little at the wonderful smell of her flowery perfume, even in all the chaos she smelt amazing.

Bettie waved over one of the waiters as he slowly came over, and with the three stars on his uniform, Graham guessed he was some sort of Chief Waiter or something.

"Please inform the kitchen, I want everything from David's Special meal quarantined until myself or Detective Adams requests it. Including food, equipment and any staff that made the food," Bettie said.

Graham leant closer to Bettie. "I think it was the wine that did it,"

Bettie's eyebrows rose. "And please quarantine

the wine David was served. Thank you,"

The Chief Waiter bowed his head slightly and went off.

Graham looked at David as he laid there on the floor in the recovery position and he vomited, coughed and struggled to breathe. This was definitely a poisoning or something, and if someone at the convention was willing to poison the head of the Federation, then Graham was really concerned about what they were willing to do to others.

Then Graham noticed David's wine glass on the floor next to David's feet and thankfully there was still some wine left in it. He knelt down and picked it up using a linen napkin.

"Do you think there's enough to run tests?" Bettie asked.

Graham nodded. He would have to drive back to Kent tonight and just hope his friend Senior Forensic Specialist Zoey Quill would be willing to run a few tests for him this late in the night.

"Zoey will find something," Graham said, "but I don't want to leave you,"

Bettie smiled. "I have Sean, and you forget I am one of the most powerful women in the Federation,"

Graham pointed to David. "And he was the most powerful man in the Federation,"

Bettie nodded. "I'll be careful, but my position would be even more in danger if I suddenly left. People would think I ran away from danger, I have to solve this,"

Graham didn't like the idea in the slightest of Bettie being here alone, but if anyone would look after her, it was definitely Sean. And despite everyone thinking he was weak because he was gay, Graham knew for a fact that was completely wrong.

"Here he is," Sean said, as two paramedics went over to David and Bettie filled them in on the situation.

Then Sean passed Graham a plastic food bag and Graham placed the wine glass and the wine inside.

Graham really wanted to have a full forensic unit examine the scene, but that wasn't going to happen. He doubted the Met police or the Kent Police for that matter would want to investigate this too quickly, more out of their own self-interest than actually protecting people. Especially as the Federation was so politically charged at the moment.

"Detective," one of the paramedics said.

Graham shook his hand. "Detective Adams. Please keep me in the loop about his condition and report your findings,"

"Of course," the paramedic said as they took David away on a stretcher.

Ivy marched over to Bettie and pulled Graham over.

"Per Federation protocols, I am Acting President Pet. And my first command is to put you two on the case, find out who poisoned the president before the criminal strikes again,"

Graham was really looking forward to this. This

was going to be great fun.

"Thanks," Bettie said, "but I have to ask. What threats has Dave been receiving?"

Ivy laughed. "Come on Pet, you know the sorts. Far-right idiots calling David a red wing crazy for allowing non-whites into the Federation. The far-left calling for David to get rid of the far-right before they destroy the Federation and then there are always the angry members who got kicked out or not licensed,"

Graham had no idea the Federation was so divided.

"What happens to the Successor and the vote?" Graham asked.

Bettie just looked at Ivy.

"Per Federation rules, David will be leaving at Closing Ceremony on Sunday. The paperwork cannot be undone until there is a legal Act of God. And… your sister is probably the only person smart enough to get through that legal mess,"

Graham and Bettie both cocked their heads.

"You know my sister isn't a lawyer, right?" Bettie asked.

Ivy smiled. "She is. She passed the Bar two weeks ago and then she's already settled three court cases,"

Graham's mouth dropped. Bettie looked equally stunned. He couldn't understand why Phryne didn't tell them?

Graham looked at Sean. He didn't know either.

"What if there isn't a successor named on Sunday?" Graham asked.

"Then," Bettie said, "I presume we would have to democratically elect a leader. Which all sensible people would want to avoid,"

"Why?" Sean asked, sounding really confused.

Ivy smiled. "Cos Pet, all the different factions of the Federation would vote for their leader. And the centrist, feminist and other -ists of the Federation thankfully have the largest fraction and their leader would win,"

Graham shrugged. "What's so wrong about having a centralist, liberal in charge?"

Bettie looked like she was almost going to laugh. "In theory, it's perfect. But that would cause the Federation to Split into the far-left, centrist and far-right organisations. We need a leader who could unite everyone. That's why David has always managed to stop the Federation from splitting,"

Graham seriously didn't think Private Eyes could be such a political bunch.

Graham kissed Bettie. "Right, I'm going to start driving back to Canterbury and I'll get Zoey to start running some tests. See you… early tomorrow morning,"

Bettie kissed him again.

Graham looked at Sean. "Don't. Leave her side,"

Sean nodded.

As Bettie left for the kitchen so he could collect whatever evidence the kitchen staff had collected. Graham felt his stomach tighten.

Something was afoot here.

Someone wanted the leadership to fall.

And the thought of Bettie being in trouble scared Graham more than he wanted to admit.

CHAPTER 7
5th August 2022
London, England

As Bettie stood on the far side of the hot boiling kitchen with long silver tables becoming hives of activity of waiters, waitresses and chefs hurried around, she realised she wasn't a fan of the heat.

She could barely see Sean who was only five metres in front of her as he was talking to a young female chef as she did some washing up.

Bettie had to admit it was great having him here, because Sean would definitely protect her no matter what, and she needed the safety of having family around after the poisoning.

It had to be a poisoning. There was no other explanation for it, but it had honestly scared Bettie. David was one of the most wonderful people in the entire world and yet someone had had the audacity to attack him.

Sure Bettie had been hearing rumours in the

Private Eye world over the past year of different political elements gaining power, but Bettie had just ignored it.

Because Private Eyes didn't use to be a political bunch. Until the last general election and the government corruption since, Bettie had known Private Eyes to focus on helping each other no matter what they believed in.

Bettie had to fix all of this, it was just a shame she knew that no one would respect a female President.

"Graham took all the food, equipment and drinks," Sean said, "that David ate. But it has to be the drink. Ten other people were served the Presidential Soup and none of them were sick,"

Bettie shook her head. She'd been expecting that, if she didn't have to have vegan food she definitely would have had the Presidential Soup. It was always the best soup she had ever tasted, and it was a real sign of respect. Since only David's personal friends could order from his menu.

That reminded Bettie of something.

"Sean, let's say you wanted to become President. Who would you target?" Bettie asked.

"Everyone who would probably get it before me. With them dead, I would most certainly get it," he said.

Bettie nodded, but she just wasn't convinced. It felt like too much of an assumption that this attack was down to the Presidency.

"What if this isn't down to the successor?" Bettie asked.

"You thinking it's political, to do with the vote or something else?" Sean asked.

Bettie gestured him to start walking out of the kitchen. They had only come in here in the first place to make sure Graham had everything and there was nothing left for them to examine.

And of course, politely ask the kitchen to hold hers and Sean's dinner order until later. To Bettie's surprise the kitchen staff jumped at the chance.

"I don't know, but it is a perfect cover," Bettie said.

Sean squeezed past two young waiters. "Definitely. If I wanted to kill someone and I wasn't interested in becoming President, I would attack during a successor announcement,"

Bettie almost crashed into a waitress carrying some soup.

"What do you know about David's other activities?" Sean asked.

"Not a lot really," Bettie said, "we talk at least once a week but that's more general stuff about how we are as people, not Private Eyes,"

"What about recently?" Sean asked.

"We've been speaking daily since the preparations of the convention have really picked up. But again that was only about the convention, nothing about threats,"

Sean pulled into a little gap between two long

silver tables where some chefs were preparing some kind of dessert.

"Does David have an office or something?" Sean asked.

Bettie smiled. "He has the presidential suite, and I'm sure our Acting President would allow us access,"

Sean smiled and they both slowly glided out of the kitchen again.

"Why didn't mum tell us she's a lawyer?" Sean asked.

Bettie was about to answer before she realised how hurt Sean sounded. She couldn't disagree, after everything Phryne had put them all through, first with her very limited acceptance of Sean being gay, all the hate she gave Bettie after becoming a Private Eye and not allowing Harry and Sean to stay with her after they were attacked and Harry got his brain injury.

Bettie seriously didn't know what was wrong with her sister.

"I don't know. Let's find her on the way up to the suite," Bettie said gently rubbing his back.

Sean simply picked up speed, and Bettie couldn't help but feel like there were so many moving pieces to this mystery that she barely knew where to begin.

But two questions were becoming very clear.

Why did David want Phryne's legal opinion in the first place?

Who was David's special guest?

Bettie hadn't seen anyone that special at the convention and that concerned her too.

What if the special guest had been attacked too?

So many attacks. So much chaos. So many moving pieces.

Bettie had to go to the Presidential Suite. Now.

CHAPTER 8
5th August 2022
Canterbury, England

Graham would never ever admit this but he was so pleased that a local judge got murdered. Because it meant that Senior Forensic Specialist Zoey Quill was still at the lab working on this wonderfully warm Friday night.

Graham was still really, really pleased that Zoey had agreed to meet with him, so he picked up a large latte for her and a very large box of doughnuts for the forensic team. Not the cheap, horrible supermarket doughnuts either, the real crispy doughnuts that had just been freshly fried.

And what made Graham even more pleased about the late hour and Zoey starting to care less and less and less about protocol regarding guests, was Graham was actually allowed inside the lab for a change.

But only a certain area.

As Graham stood in the far corner leaning on a freezing cold metal lab with tons of expensive, high-tech equipment around him, Graham watched Zoey and her team in their long white coats as they finished up in another room.

Graham had neatly laid out all the evidence on the metal table for them to examine. And Graham knew that Bettie would be pleased at his neatness, because the evidence clearly flowed from the least to most possible thing used to deliver the poison.

It's a shame Bettie wasn't here to see it, Graham really hoped she was okay.

It was amazing to see them all work like the experts they were, Graham wouldn't have a clue how to run the advance tests they were doing, but then again that's probably what they thought about his policing.

After all when a criminal is running towards you with a knife, what do you do? Lots of people would freeze, Graham would not.

After a few more moments, Zoey came through the small metal door that separated Graham from the rest of Zoey's team, and Zoey's face lit up when she saw the doughnuts and latte on the table.

Then she frowned when she saw the evidence.

"You always did know how to delight and disappoint a girl," Zoey said with a smile.

Graham just blushed. "Here's the evidence from the poisoning I phoned about,"

Zoey nodded and slowly looked at the evidence.

"I think there are three pieces of evidence that are the most likely to contain the poison," Graham said.

Zoey smiled as she picked up David's wine glass. Graham wondered if she was judging him for putting it in a plastic food bag.

Zoey slowly opened it and got out some cotton swabs and started to take samples.

"Who was the victim?" Zoey asked.

"One of Bettie's friends. The President of the British Private Eye Federation," Graham said.

"A very good man then," Zoey said, as she placed the cotton swab in a very high-tech looking machine.

"You knew him?"

"Yes, a few years back there was a Forensic Convention year and David was doing a talk on the effects of weather on dead bodies,"

Graham cocked his head. "How did he know about that?"

"Private Eyes are a broad church Graham. Some find dead bodies, some make them and others, like Bettie, focus on helping people,"

"What type was David?" Graham asked.

The machine beeped and Zoey walked over to it and shook her head.

"There's no poison in the wine glass. It's your normal expensive wine for posh wine snobs," Zoey said.

Graham frowned. He had really been hoping that

was the murder weapon.

"Okay," Graham said. Then he picked up a large saucepan that contained the Presidential Soup that David had been eating before he vomited.

Zoey took out the swabs again, collected samples and got the machine to run them.

"My question," Graham said.

"Oh yes," Zoey said, "I met the man once at a convention Graham. I don't know him perfectly. But he seemed like a great man, he was probably just like Bettie. A Private Eye who wanted to help people,"

Graham didn't know how true that was actually. He didn't know how much a person was a Private Eye once they become President, there was a chance David hadn't solved any cases for decades.

Graham had to find out.

The machine beeped.

"Nope," Zoey said. "No poison whatsoever,"

Graham shook his head. It shouldn't be this hard to find some poison.

"Here," Graham said, as he passed Zoey the knife, fork and spoon David had been used.

Again she got out her cotton swabs, collected samples and got the machine to run them.

Graham didn't have too much hope because it didn't seem logical for the cutlery to be poisoned.

"If there was an opening for the new Head of Forensics at Kent Police how dangerous would the competition get?" Graham asked.

Zoey laughed. "Not in the slightest. I'm basically

head of Forensics at Canterbury in all but name. It would probably be me and some other people up for the job. But I don't want to leave Canterbury yet,"

Graham smiled. "You just love working with me, don't you?"

Zoey laughed. "You are one of my favourite Detectives. But it's them. I really love them,"

Graham watched Zoey as she pointed to her team, and Graham completely understood it. He loved working with Bettie, Sean and anyone else he got to work with regularly. He wouldn't want to give any of them up, not even for a second.

The machine beeped.

Zoey laughed hard. "Nope. No poison,"

"Can you check again?" Graham asked.

Zoey shook her head but stopped. "Oh,"

"What?" Graham asked.

"Well there's this chemical that shouldn't be in the soup. It's tasteless but the amount of it is strange,"

"What chemical?" Graham asked.

"It's too hard to say but I know this chemical is normally used in tri-poisons,"

Graham frowned. He had heard of these types of poisons before and he hated the sound of them. It was a poison that was made up of three separate and completely safe ingredients. What made the poison deadly was when the three ingredients were combined inside a person.

Zoey looked at the results from the saucepan and

the wine glass.

"Just as I thought," she said, "each element contains an ingredient of a very well-known tri-poison,"

Graham felt his stomach tense. Whoever had poisoned David had to be very clever and really know their way around poisons. He never would have come up with tri-poisons by himself.

The criminal was clearly clever.

That really concerned Graham.

Bettie and Sean were alone. In a convention hotel.

With a clever poisoner.

Graham had to get back there. Now!

CHAPTER 9
6th August 2022
London, England

Bettie wasn't too pleased she was still up at midnight, but she owned it to David to find out what had happened. And most importantly who the hell was behind it.

Thankfully Ivy had managed to get the guests, fellow Private Eyes and wannabes away from the dining room and into the conference chamber for the evening games, drinks and partying.

No one seemed to care about the change.

Yet Bettie couldn't understand why she couldn't find Phryne. She had asked all the twenty bar people at the hotel. No one had seen her and she wasn't in her room, it was so strange.

But Bettie had to help David first.

Bettie opened the golden door to David's Presidential Suite and was instantly stunned by the amazingness of it all. She had expected wonderful furniture, lights and cushions but this was something else.

The Presidential Suite was massive and just the living area was probably a hundred metres squared. Bettie loved the massive sofas that were in front of a 100 inch TV and a great gas fireplace in the middle.

And right next to Bettie was a large drinks cabinet, Bettie recognised some of the labels on the bottles. This was the extremely good stuff that most mere mortals could only dream about tasting.

No wonder David chose this hotel for the convention. They knew how to treat their guests.

Even the room smelt stunning with refreshing hints of lemon, lime and mint that created the most welcoming aroma Bettie had experienced in ages, and Bettie did enjoy the taste of Italian ice cream it left on her tongue.

"Auntie," Sean said passing Bettie a very large vegan chocolate bar.

"Thanks," Bettie said, putting it in her pocket. She was definitely going to need it soon.

"Is there an office or something?" Sean asked.

Bettie didn't have a clue. This place was so massive she was more concerned about getting lost.

"I don't know. Spread out and let's see," Bettie said.

Sean walked right out in front of her. "Seriously?"

Bettie rolled her eyes. "Spread out. No one will attack me in the Presidential Suite,"

"And how many cocky presidents all over the world have thought the same?" Sean asked smiling.

Bettie playfully pushed him away and they both laughed.

Bettie found a bright white door in along of the impressively painted walls that looked more like a work of art rather than a hotel wall. She opened it and started to walk down it.

This little walkway easily went on for another hundred metres and Bettie was really surprised to see the massive bedrooms with its silk sheets, Egyptian cotton towels and ethically-sourced duck feathered pillows. This place was amazing.

Then Bettie saw a few bathrooms the size of sheds and even more hot tubs than she realised was possible.

Each hot tub could probably fit fifty people inside.

"Found anything else!" Sean shouted.

"No," Bettie said.

Bettie kept walking along until she opened a large black door than revealed the most stunning view she had ever seen. In the suite's office, there were massive floor-to-ceiling windows that allowed Bettie to see all of the breath-taking landmarks of London.

It was beautiful.

Bettie heard someone walk in behind her.

Bettie tensed.

She spun around.

Raising her fists.

Sean shot back.

"It's me!" Sean shouted.

"Sorry," Bettie said feeling really bad.

"So this has to be his office," Sean said.

Bettie nodded as she tore herself away from the stunning view and focused on the solid gold marble of the desk that was easily the size of most single beds. It was extraordinary.

Bettie went over and started to look through the draws. Sean did the same on the other end.

"Try to find his laptop," Bettie said.

"Did you know anything about this law change?" Sean asked.

Bettie shook her head. That was something that was bothering her, both as a friend and a Private Eye.

She had absolutely no problem with the law change itself because it was utterly ridiculous the amount of untrained people that went around pretending to be professional Private Eyes, breaking the law and then other people moaning that Private Eyes were criminal rogues.

She absolutely hated those people. To be a Private Eye Bettie firmly believed a person should have to be trained and licensed to be able to practice, something that the current UK law failed on.

Bettie knew Scotland had tried to introduce a legal requirement for Private Eyes to be a member of the Federation, but the UK government had firmly called that idea unlawful and forced Scotland to remove it. Bettie still had a problem with the government because of that.

And the UK would be a lot safer if only professional Private Eyes were allowed to work, just like how professionally trained cops, doctors and psychologists were only allowed to practice after jumping through a bunch of hoops.

But what really bothered her was David didn't come to her for her advice. It might have sounded petty as anything but Bettie already believed David valued her opinion. Well, she knew that was true, it was just so strange that he didn't ask her this time.

"No I didn't know anything about it," Bettie said to Sean.

"My only concern was," Sean asked, "can this be used to disadvantage certain groups?"

Bettie just looked at Sean. "Please don't say that in public. Between you and me, perfectly fine. Just do not say that in public. The Federation had the discussion before and… it was messy,"

Bettie seriously never wanted the Federation to have to relook at that argument.

The entire point of the Federation's training requirements was they were meant to be hard. Because as everyone saw it, it wasn't an automatic right for a person to be a Private Eye, it had to be earned.

And you have to know a hell of a lot of things before the Federation would even consider licensing you.

Bettie opened a draw that smelt of wonderful

cinnamon, saw nothing was in there and closed it.

Then one day, a young woman from a very poor part of England got rejected and Bettie felt so sorry for her. But instead of learning more like the Broad of Membership had recommended, the young woman decided to call it discrimination.

Now Bettie knew for a fact, it was extremely, extremely rare for women, gay people and any minority group to play a card. But it seriously annoyed Bettie when they did, because it didn't help anyone.

So the young woman took it to court, there was fighting within the Federation and everyone was pissed with each other. Bettie still admired the hell out of David for how he handled it.

"But no Sean," Bettie said, "I promise you the requirements are fair,"

Sean nodded as he opened the very bottom draw on his side.

"Found it!" Sean shouted.

Bettie smiled as she jumped up and went over to him.

Bettie was really pleased to see David's very expensive and secure laptop perfectly in place. Bettie opened it and typed in his passwords that David had shared with her yesterday.

Then Sean took over being the computer expert when Harry wasn't about, and searched for the most recent things accessed.

Sean's eyebrows rose. "Auntie, what's the Private

Republic of Private Eyes?"

Bettie rolled her eyes. That was one name she did not want to hear again.

"It's a far-far-right split off organisation from the Federation. They never actually split off but they threatened to during the Brexit Referendum because it was apparently disgusting that David was allowing non-whites into the Federation,"

"David accessed all the old files on the group last night. And then there were three names he searched up before he shut down his laptop,"

"What names?" Bettie asked.

"Joanna Green. Johnny Gray. Grayson Lange," Sean said.

Bettie just shook her head. They were three of the worse troublemakers and more political people in the entire federation. It was actually those three enemies that had made the Federation so political in recent years.

"So David searches up an old hate group, searches for three names and then gets poisoned," Bettie said.

Sean nodded. "I've sent all this to your laptop in case we need it later,"

"Thank you. We need to see those three,"

"Start off with Johnny?" Sean asked with a smile.

Bettie frowned. "I'm not taking you as a gay person there, and I'm not going there as a pregnant woman. Graham will deal with that foul git,"

Sean looked shocked at Bettie. Bettie wasn't

kidding.

But if those people were involved. Something massive was going on.

Something that would easily destroy the Federation.

And hurt everyone she loved.

CHAPTER 10
6th August 2022
London, England

Wow!

Graham had never slept in such an amazingly soft bed in all his life. No wonder the hotel cost so much per night, but Graham had loved it. He felt so full of youthful energy that he honestly felt as if he could conquer the world, fight evil and do anything he wanted to.

Graham and Bettie had originally wanted to split, and Graham definitely wanted to have a private chat with this Johnny idiot, he hated women feeling unsafe and he wasn't going to have this far-right nutter mistreating anyone, especially Bettie and Sean.

But after asking around, it turned out that both Johnny and Joanna were at the same place, the conference chamber.

Graham was rather surprised when him and Bettie got down there at the sheer scale of it all. It was massive yesterday with all the stalls, people chatting and everything else. But now all the people who arrived last night were here, it easily added another five hundred people.

The entire convention chamber was filled with deafening noise as everyone's talking, shouting and laughing rolled into one constant sound.

Graham looked at the main stage where the Opening Ceremony and Bettie's first panel was held, and Graham was a bit surprised to see a group of people crowded around presumably Johnny and Joanna screaming at each other as loud as they could.

Graham and Bettie slowly wondered over, and Graham had honestly expected Johnny to be taller and posher and just better. As far as Graham was concerned, Johnny was nothing more than a middle-aged man with pale skin, tons of nationalist tattoos and horrible black teeth.

In other words, he was the stereotypical nationalist.

But Joanna definitely wasn't… stereotypical. As far as Graham was aware, he always imagined far-left people to be pompous, a little arrogant and a little unhinged around the edges because they believed in completely tearing down the capitalist system and recreating the world.

Joanna looked nothing like that with her long brown hair, perfect little summer dress and movie star smile. Now Graham definitely understood why some of the men were staring at her, and not the fight itself.

"You bitch face pig!" Johnny shouted.

Graham just smiled because it was always amazing to see politically-motivated fights because they really were so pointless.

And from what Graham could understand in amongst all the deafening noise was Johnny was attacking Joanna because she was a woman, and according to Johnny the only place for a woman was in the kitchen with her white husband and their children.

Graham just laughed and looked at Bettie. He enjoyed Bettie being out and about, and in all honesty his stomach would absolutely hate her being in the kitchen full-time.

Some of her meals were… well, calling them meals was an insult.

"Don't worry hun," Bettie said smiling, "I won't be in the kitchen any time soon,"

Graham mockingly wiped his forehead. Bettie playfully hit him.

"Stop this!" Bettie shouted as her and Graham forced their way through the crowd.

"Oh wow. Another bitch face slut," Johnny said.

Graham actually gasped. That was probably the worst thing someone had ever called Bettie, and Graham knew she had been called a lot over the decades.

"That's enough everyone," Graham said shooing away the fight's audience.

Johnny walked over to Bettie. Graham firmly

stood in front of her.

"You know mate," Johnny said to Graham, "you better get rid of her soon. Once a woman's pregnant she better be bed-bound or put down,"

"Back. Off. Now!" Graham said firmly.

"You don't believe me. Shame. That's the problem with women, there's such stupid creatures and we can't even cage them up anymore. That's why this country went to pot,"

Graham seriously had no clue why David hadn't expelled him from the Federation.

"And you think becoming President will help you?" Graham asked.

Johnny smiled. "I tell you this my mate comrade. In the war against oppression from women, we cannot give them any safe spaces. When I'm President, woman Private Eyes will be a thing of the past,"

Graham really wanted to punch him.

"Would you get rid of David to make that happen?" Graham asked.

Johnny laughed.

"Listen mate," Johnny said, "I don't know what rubbish your slut's been telling you, but I ain't no killer. Men will win the war through peaceful means. Men aren't savages that feel the need to smash up shop windows to get their power,"

Johnny laughed and just walked away.

Graham wanted to ask him a few more questions, and he really wanted to correct Johnny and mention that it was only the minority of women who did that, and the only reason the suffragettes did that in the first place was because men didn't listen to them.

But Graham knew it was flat out useless, just like Johnny.

Bettie's amazingly musical laugh made Graham turn around and smile as he watched Bettie and Joanna laughing their heads off.

Graham went over to them. "You two okay?"

Bettie tried to catch her breath. "Yes, it's just a few Private Eye jokes,"

"How was talking to *him*?" Joanna asked.

Graham didn't know how to take that, he had been expecting some foul language, hate or something else from Joanna. But sure she seemed annoyed but not hateful.

"I'm sorry," Graham said, "but are you actually far-left?"

Joanna smiled. "What? You mean a revolutionary that wants to rebuild the world, redistribute wealth towards the poor and punish the evil political elites that oppress us?"

Graham nodded slowly. He didn't want to seem too against it just in case she did attack him.

Joanna laughed. "Na. Sure I'm left-wing, but I literally just want a government that cares and wants to protect the working-class, and isn't more interested in protecting the rich and powerful and the corrupt compared to us working people,"

Graham nodded. That would definitely be nice.

"Sorry," Graham said, "just… just didn't know what things to avoid,"

Joanna nodded and gestured Bettie and Graham to walk with her.

"What can I help you both with?" Joanna asked as they glided through a crowd of speakers for the first panel of the day.

"I overheard," Graham said, "someone mention you planned to get rid of the Far-right,"

"Seriously?" Joanna said. "In the Federation, I am technically the leader of the political left simply because my dad's a labour MP. Great man and I do support his politics,"

"But you don't make politic arguments or use the Federation to further politics?" Bettie asked.

Jonna sort of shook her head as the three of them ducked into a little offshoot towards some stalls away from the main area of the convention.

"No. I used the Federation to moan about Brexit. Yes. But I don't use the Federation for that anymore, I promise, and if I made the Federation political. I am really sorry for that," Joanna said.

She started coughing.

"You okay?" Graham asked.

"Yea, just got a tickle in my throat,"

Graham nodded. That was a relief.

"This overheard plan then?" Graham asked.

"As I said, my father is a great MP and sometimes I joke I want to get rid of the far-right elements in the Federation. Especially with them growing in number, influence and power,"

Graham didn't know that, and judging by Bettie grabbing his hand, she didn't either.

"But no Bet," Joanna said, "I'm not going to do anything against them. And in my element's monthly newsletter I always tell them not to do anything. The vote is how we get power, not violence,"

Joanna coughed again.

"Can I get you some water?" Bettie asked.

"Yes please," Joanna said.

Bettie left to get some water.

Graham looked at Joanna. "Do you-"

Joanna vomited.

All over Graham.

She collapsed to the ground.

She couldn't breathe.

The criminal struck again.

CHAPTER 11
6th August 2022
London, England

As Bettie watched the paramedics take Joanna away in a horribly clinical stretcher with a mini-ventilator forced down her throat, she was really starting to hate this poisoner, whoever they were.

The constant deafening noise of everyone talking, shouting and laughing filled the convention chamber, as did everyone's horrid scent of sweat, expensive aftershave and whatever else people felt the need to wear. Bettie didn't like all the strange smells, or maybe that was first her over-sensitive pregnant body trying to protect her.

But what really concerned Bettie was how close she had been to Joanna when she was poisoned, and it was so strange how Joanna hadn't been eating or drinking or touching anything when she fell.

The paramedics had sadly said Joanna would remain on a ventilator for the foreseeable future because the poison had almost killed her outright.

That was the scary thing.

Unlike David's poisoning this time the killer had almost killed Joanna, so clearly the criminal was upping their game, so Bettie had to up her game too.

"Graham," Bettie said, "drive back to Canterbury please and collect Zoey. Tell her we have the equipment she needs and the Federation will pay her two thousand pounds if she works for us today and tomorrow,"

Graham frowned. Bettie wondered if he was doubting her ability to make such a commitment, especially with a new President coming in tomorrow, one that may not like seeing such an expense so soon.

"Relax, I'll make Ivy do the bank transfer today so it isn't the new President's problem," Bettie said.

Graham didn't look convinced. "Just stay safe,"

Bettie kissed him and watched his amazing ass as Graham glided through the crowd away.

"What is all the chaos!" Phryne shouted behind Bettie.

Bettie turned around and was really pleased to see Sean escorting Phryne over to her.

Bettie gestured them to follow her and Bettie wanted to lead them towards one of the storage rooms where they could talk very privately.

"Where have you been?" Bettie asked Phryne.

Sean laughed, but Bettie noticed there were hints of anger in his voice.

"I was... dealing with someone," Phryne said.

Bettie stopped and spun around. "Don't tell me you were doing someone. You're married,"

Phryne smiled. "Well that Johnny is a very charming man,"

"Fucking hell," Bettie said and she simply walked on.

She might not have been the biggest fan of Sean's dad John, but it was ridiculous that Phryne had had an affair and did someone on the side.

It was even worse that it was the far-right idiot Johnny Gray. And Bettie still didn't know why David had ran a search for those three names before he was poisoned.

Sean walked next to Bettie. He too furious.

Up ahead Bettie saw one of the storage rooms so she went inside and gestured Sean and Phryne to follow her.

Bettie was rather impressed by the massive size of the storage room. It looked more like a small meeting room and definitely not a room meant to be used for storage.

Bettie just looked at Phryne. "What the hell were you thinking!"

Phryne folded her arms. "I'm sorry if my life hasn't been perfect of late,"

Sean stood firmly next to Bettie. "What do you mean? I've called you tons of times. I've wanted to help you mum. I've wanted to know if you were okay,"

Bettie just shook her head. There was clearly

something those two weren't telling them.

"What's going on?" Bettie asked.

Phryne rolled her eyes. "With Sean and Harry being beaten, Harry having brain damage and John being... not there. I don't know what I'm meant to do,"

Bettie hugged her sister. "You talk to us. We're your family. We have always been there for you,"

"It's you that just pushed us away," Sean said bitterly.

Bettie realised what was going on and she really should have seen it sooner. Ever since the attack and Harry's brain damage, the two boyfriends had been living with her and Graham, and Phryne hadn't been in contact too much.

Bettie had wanted to say it was strange, but she just thought Phryne needed time to deal with her child being attacked. But clearly Sean hadn't wanted Bettie's support at first, he had wanted the love and support of his mother.

Something that never came.

Bettie looked Phryne dead in the eye. "We will deal with this later, but you two will talk and you Phryne will not avoid your son. But I need to know something first,"

Phryne frowned. "What?"

"Why did David want you here?" Bettie asked.

Phryne threw her arms up in the air. "He wanted to make an Article change so the rules that governed the Federation allowed him to do something,"

"What?" Sean asked still annoyed.

"He wanted to still be a member of the Federation even after quitting,"

"But that isn't happening," Bettie said, "the Federation rules are clear on that matter. Once a President leaves, they're leaving the Federation for good,"

Phryne smiled. "He wanted to change that rule because he was concerned about something. Something about theft of Federation funds and something known as Article 20 and 66,"

Bettie hadn't expected that to come up in the slightest, those two articles were what the Federation secretly called their blackmail articles. It was a massive collection of government and police corruption that spread back to 1910.

It was the Federation's fail safe in case any government wanted to destroy the Federation and attack Private Eyes. It was also a last line of defence in case a police officer wanted to destroy an innocent Private Eye.

Just the threat of using those Articles had saved Bettie from a life in prison for fake charges a few months ago.

"How could they be stolen?" Bettie asked.

Phryne took a step closer. "I don't know. The only thing he mentioned was he didn't want the wrong person to become President,"

Bettie shook her head. "What? He was concerned the next President would destroy the blac… the Articles,"

Bettie almost revealed what they actually were. She couldn't allow that, not even to her own family.

Phryne shrugged.

Maybe Bettie had been right in the first place, maybe this was about something bigger than the Presidency and about something a lot more fundamental.

Because if those Articles were stolen. Then the Federation would be easy pickings to its political enemies.

Leading to the destruction of the Federation itself.

And all Private Eyes would be vulnerable.

That terrified Bettie.

Her, her friends and every Private Eye's livelihood and freedom was at stake.

Bettie couldn't fail.

CHAPTER 12
6th August 2022
London, England

It had actually been a lot easier to convince Zoey to come than Graham had ever thought possible. He had been expecting tons of protests, something about wanting to spend more time with her kids and generally just not wanting to work at the weekend.

But it turned out the kids were at their grandparents for the weekend and Zoey's husband had been called away on emergency classified business. So Zoey was home alone.

Needless to say, she jumped at the chance to work and Graham was really pleased.

As Graham stood in a small little room with posh oak panels covering the walls and grand expensive paintings that he expected to see in art galleries and not a little forgotten room, he was starting to wonder what else the Federation was hiding.

When Bettie had mentioned they had all the

equipment Zoey would need to run tests, he had expected a few old machines, maybe a few grumpy salespeople and even some former-lab techs to help Zoey.

But nope.

The Federation had some of the top companies in the world here trying to sell Private Eyes their forensic equipment. And what amazed Graham even more, was tons of people were shelling out the half a million pounds needed for the equipment, if he hadn't already known how much Bettie made, he would have been seriously jealous.

So the Federation bought the equipment for Zoey like it was nothing.

The machine beeped and the quiet groan of the deafening crowd outside barely filtered through the walls as Zoey looked at the results of a half-eaten chocolate bar from Joanna's pocket.

"Just as before," Zoey said, "the chocolate bar contains one element of a very well-known duo-poison,"

Graham shook his head. This wasn't what they needed, he had been hoping at the very least the poisoner had been using the same poison as before. But it was becoming clear the poisoner was becoming more and more sophisticated. Moving from tri- to duo poisons.

"Anyway to know the other ingredient?" Graham asked.

"Yes but it's common. The other ingredient can

be found in most perfumes," Zoey said.

"So all this poisoner needed was to given Joanna the poisoned chocolate bar and let the poison in that react with the perfume on her skin,"

Zoey nodded. "You know, this requires very specific knowledge. You don't find this in a university textbook, class or anything very common. I only have a basic understanding of this because of a conference I went…"

Graham clicked his fingers. "The conference David spoke at?"

Zoey nodded.

Graham took out his phone, logged into his police databases and started to look up that conference. He was really interested in the other guests from the Federation.

"Where's Bettie, Sean and Phryne?" Zoey asked.

Graham smiled. "Bettie decided it was best if Sean and Phryne had a heart-to-heart,"

"I know the feeling," Zoey said.

Graham wondered if she was just being dismissive like people normally were when they said 'I know how you feel' when they learn their relative got murdered, but there was such a hint of kindness to Zoey's words.

Graham finished typing in a search, let it run and went over to Zoey.

"What you mean? If you don't mind me asking,"

Zoey frowned. "My brother. Used to be such a great young man, he was five years older than me. He loved life, work and girls. He was…"

Zoey took a very deep breath.

"He was driving home from work one night. Wasn't speeding or anything. Just driving home, when a lorry jumped a light and smashed into him. My brother had massive brain damage, he still couldn't speak today nor get dressed by himself,"

Graham didn't know what to say.

"My mother took to drugs, sex and alcohol. My father got too depressed for months and there I was… barely 18 years old and I had to look after my brother, take him to therapy and everything else,"

Graham really felt for her. "How did you cope?"

Zoey looked like she was about to cry. "I didn't. I don't really talk to my parents now. My brother is in a specialist place and I visit at least once a week. But your situation can be better,"

Graham accidentally grabbed her arm like a starving person like grab a chance to have food.

Then Graham realised what he was doing and he released her arm.

"I'm sorry. How do me and Bettie help?" Graham asked.

"You do what you're doing. I would have loved to have an aunt or something to move in with. It would have been better than watching my parents be useless as I looked after my brother,"

Graham bit his lip.

"And you keep showing Sean he isn't alone and that you love him. He's already been doing that, and then you to get Sean and Phryne to talk,"

Graham nodded.

"Because I'll tell you this now. Right now, Sean feels like a victim. He might not know it, but he does. He probably feels like it's his fault for the attack and his parents are taking out their anger on him for being who is he, and that's why they're abandoning him and not letting him move back in,"

Graham could only nod. It was so strange that Phryne had never contacted Sean, Bettie or him about Sean and Harry moving in with them. Granted, Graham and Bettie loved having them around but it was still strange.

Graham's phone beeped. The search was done.

"Grayson Lange," Graham said. "That was the only person from the Federation that attended that conference with David,"

"And he would have attended the same talks as David. Or he might have got to the duo and tri-poison talks alone,"

Graham went to go and get Bettie, but Zoey was right. Sean and Phryne had to talk this out, so he looked at Zoey.

"Want to confront a possible poisoner?" Graham said, smiling.

"Of course Detective Adams. I thought you would never ask,"

Graham and Zoey stormed out of the room.

He had to stop Grayson Lange before he hurt anyone else.

And before he hurt anyone he loved.

CHAPTER 13
6th August 2022
London, England

Bettie just stood there in the very posh meeting/storage room as she watched Sean and Phryne talk it out, shout and even swear at each other as they sat on very comfortable metal chairs.

Bettie had never seen Phryne so defensive and angry and rageful at anyone, even back when they were children. The most angry Bettie had seen Phryne was probably when they were sixteen and Bettie may or may not have stolen a boy off her sister.

Phryne had been fuming at them, but she quickly changed her tune when that same boy humiliated Bettie at their secondary school prom.

Yet as Bettie just watched Phryne get more and more and more defensive as she explained how hard she was finding every one, how she never really wanted a gay son because she actually wanted biological grandchildren, and she hated his father

John flying around for his job. Bettie really started to feel like she didn't know her sister as well as she believed.

Bettie had always tried to be a great sister to Phryne, but Phryne had never truly respected her becoming a Private Eye, making tons of money and finding love with Graham.

Part of that was probably because Phryne had had Sean so young, and as Phryne never failed to remind anyone when she was drunk (which was becoming more and more common) she never wanted kids so early. She wanted a life first.

"Just leave me alone Sean. Let me live a little you ungrateful kid," Phryne said as she went towards the door.

Sean just sat there. Not crying. Not smiling. Not anything.

Then all three of their phones buzzed and even the deafening talking, laughing and shouting outside fell silent.

Bettie and Sean just looked at each other.

They all took out their phones and Bettie realised all her Private Eye and non-Private Eye friends had texted, emailed and tried to call her all saying the same thing- *is this your sister?*

And it included a link.

Bettie clicked the link and to her utter horror, it was a sex tape between Johnny Gray and Phryne. It had been uploaded to all the porn, news and social media sites with one message playing over and over again.

This is Phryne, a highly respected lawyer from a major UK law firm. But you all, given the chance all women will revert back to their rightful place, their slutty place. Remember men, women are oppressing us. We cannot allow the sluts to continue!

Bettie was absolutely horrified. This was outrageous that Johnny could do this. But Bettie couldn't help but smile out of utter shock, the situation wasn't funny in the slightest.

But it was amazing that some idiot would actually do this.

Bettie just looked at Sean, who was frowning at Phryne. He looked so furious, pissed and so hurt.

Then Bettie went over to Phryne who was crying her eyes out. Phryne's phone buzzed from her boss.

Bettie took the phone and answered.

"Phryne's Office, how may I help you?" Bettie said.

"Please tell Phryne that her services are no longer required. Due to the Public Embarrassment Clause in her employment contract, she has been terminated. A Sacking payment of an additional three thousand pounds will be sent today, in addition, to her remaining unpaid wages. Good day,"

Bettie looked at Phryne who was standing right behind her. She snatched her phone and ran off.

"She doesn't deserve that," Sean said behind Bettie.

Bettie turned around. She wanted to say

something comforting to Sean, but she had no words whatsoever. Phryne had just been shamed in the worse possible way.

"We need to deal with Johnny," Bettie said.

"Legally?" Sean said, an evil smile forming on his face.

"Ideally. But I think discrediting him will be enough. I'll handle Johnny but I think you should go back to Canterbury," Bettie said.

Sean folded his arms. "Why? Don't you want me now?"

Then Sean must have realised what he said, he threw his arms around Bettie. Bettie just wanted to fix everything, but from what Phryne had been saying through their arguments, and Sean trying to just talk calmly. This was all down to Phryne just wanting a bit of freedom away from family, children and her husband.

As far as Bettie was concerned Phryne could have it, when she gave birth next month, she was never ever going to treat her children like this.

Bettie clicked her fingers. "David was poisoned. Joanna was poisoned. Phryne was shamed,"

Sean nodded.

"What if everything is connected?" Bettie asked, "come to think of it. The Private Republic of Private eyes did form in a way back around the Brexit Referendum, and one of their core principles was all feminists, women and etc must die,"

Sean tried to look surprised, but both Bettie and

Sean knew better than most the hate certain groups experienced on a daily basis. Bettie had never liked the Private republic, thankfully it was so small in number, but one of Joanna's comments really concerned her.

The number of far-right people in the Federation was growing.

So what if Bettie, Ivy and Graham had been flat out wrong?

Bettie nodded at that. It made perfect sense in a way, if the number of far-right people did increase in the Federation and David couldn't announce a successor. Then it made sense why they would want an election, because Johnny Gray would certainly get elected to be the new President.

That was not a fun idea.

And what if David had been wrong in his assumption of someone wanting to steal Article 20 and 66? What if they wanted to use it instead to blackmail the government and police so the far-right couldn't be prosecuted and over time a far-right government could be installed?

It sounded so far-fetched, so Bettie knew it was possible.

Back in all the chaos around the requirements being too tough, Bettie had had conversations with David about the possibility of a President abusing the protection Article 20 and 66 gave them.

David had tried to deny it all, but they agreed it was definitely possible. There had been a few documented instances, like back in the Second World War, the Federation had blackmailed some government sources who refused to give the military the money needed to fund the D-Day operation that ultimately freed the world.

So it was possible for the Federation to control, or at least influence the government in some small but very meaningful ways.

Johnny Gray had to be involved.

He had to be stopped.

This wasn't just about the livelihood of Private Eyes.

This was about national security.

And Bettie would stop it.

No matter what.

CHAPTER 14
6th August 2022
London, England

Graham was definitely not impressed with Grayson Lange as he stared at what remained of Grayson at the hotel bar completely drunk and almost unconscious.

The hotel bar itself was amazing with its very expensive and posh alcohol, Victorian-styled chairs and bar area made from the finest oak one could find. But Graham hated to see their suspect completely drunk and unable to answer their questions.

Graham watched the bar woman who was wearing a very tight waitress suit-like uniform as she fixed some cocktails for a group of female Private Eyes who was were sitting nearby talking, laughing and having a great time.

Graham might have had a case to solve, but it was great to see people enjoying themselves. He truly believed that it was the small victories and positive things like that that kept whatever darkness the world had at bay.

Zoey stood next to Graham as she returned from getting changed quickly, and Graham was seriously impressed with her. She was wearing the most stunning flowery summer dress he had ever seen. She looked so young, beautiful and really attractive.

Graham went over to the barwoman and showed her his badge.

"Detective Adams Kent Police," he said.

"Kent? Are you lost deary, this is London," the barwoman said smiling.

"What can you tell me about the drunk there?" Graham said pointing towards Grayson.

The barwoman poured various alcohols into a cocktail shaker.

"Not a lot. He's been in here since the morning. He started off on rum and coke spoke to lots of… not very nice people. They pinched my ass, grabbed my boobs a few times and then I switched him to another drink. Clearly he couldn't handle as much as he thought,"

Zoey gave her a little round of applause. Graham knew from personal experience never ever to drink mix once you're had something strong like rum. That was always a very bad idea.

"He hasn't left at all?" Graham asked. "Did you see him give any of the men anything?"

The barwoman poured the cocktail into some glasses and passed them to the woman at the other end of the bar.

"Nope. He didn't leave. He didn't give anyone anything," she said, starting to make two more drinks.

Graham just looked at Zoey. He had at least been hoping he had given someone anything that could have contained the poison.

"Excuse me," Zoey said, "do you sell chocolate bars?"

The barwoman shook her head as she finished up making two drinks the colour of cola.

"Here you go," she said, "two virgin rum and cokes,"

Graham cocked his head.

"For my time," the barwoman said smiling.

Graham laughed and passed her some cash before quickly grabbing Zoey and walking quickly away.

"Why are walking so quickly?" Zoey asked.

"I gave her some monopoly money," Graham said.

He quickly looked behind her, and the barwoman didn't even seem to notice.

"I guess we need to look at this," Zoey said, subtly passing Graham, Grayson's phone.

Graham carefully guided Zoey back into the convention chamber and he was suddenly hit with all the awful loud talking, joking and shouting again, along with the awful smell of sweat.

Zoey tilted the phone upwards so she could see where Grayson's fingers had been touching. Then she typed in her first guess.

Nothing.

But Graham frowned when he saw a warning pop up about the phone being erased if the password was entered wrong two more times.

Zoey tried again.

Nothing.

"Maybe we should ask around for a phone unlocker," Graham said.

Zoey laughed. She tried again. The phone unlocked.

"Look at this…" Graham said, wanting Zoey to look at his messages, but a video popped up.

It seemed to be a video of Phryne and Johnny Gray doing each other hard, and it seemed like Grayson was somehow running a computer programme that uploaded it onto as many websites as the software could find.

"What is this?" Zoey asked.

Graham really wanted to make some bad comment about Phryne and her awful choices, but this clearly wasn't the time. And it was outrageous for this to happen to any woman, regardless of their choices.

Zoey pulled up Grayson's messages. He had deleted all of them, except three. One was from his mother (that was just sad), the second set of messages was probably from his girlfriend but Grayson was enough of a scumbag to simply label her contact as "Bimbo" and the third was a lot more interesting.

The third set of messages was from a Social Media group termed *The Private Republic of Supreme Private Eyes*.

Most of the messages were just hard to read. They were so hateful, uninformed and twisted every logical argument a person could make in favour of equality. This was outrageous.

But the very last message caught Graham's eyes.

"The first English Sister Slut is dealt with. Move onto Plan B-ettie," Zoey said slowly.

Graham felt his stomach twist into an extremely painful knot. Sweat started to pour down his forehead, back and chest.

Johnny and his friends were going to move against her.

Graham couldn't allow them.

He had to find Bettie.

Now!

CHAPTER 15
6th August 2022
London, England

Bettie leant against the wonderfully cold wooden bar that had been prepared and made-up in the convention chamber, so many of the stalls and other things had been taken down quickly to create a much larger space for tonight's Annual General Meeting.

Bettie watched as people sat, spoke and sneered at others at their little wooden tables that were poshly arranged in long sweeping rows that formed a perfect rectangle in front of the main stage.

"Where's Ivy?"

Bettie had heard a few people ask that and it was actually a fair question. Bettie hadn't seen Ivy for a while, and considering she was Acting President she should have been here a while ago to start preparing for the Vote tonight.

A strong muscular arm wrapped round Bettie and Bettie kissed Graham as him and Sean came over to her.

"I told you to be careful," Graham said.

Bettie smiled and rolled her eyes. All she was doing was getting a drink before the voting, arguments and whatever else was going to happen started, it wasn't like she was going to get poisoned, attacked or whatever in front of all these people.

But she knew she was wrong about that, the poisoner had already striked twice in front of people, so clearly the criminal wanted to be seen and they wanted people to remember their deeds.

Maybe that was a lot more important than Bettie had realised earlier.

"Here you go Miss English," the barman said with a drink as he passed Bettie her diet coke.

Graham went to take the drink, but Bettie pulled it away from him. As much as she loved him, she couldn't help but feel like he was taking this all too seriously, or she wasn't.

The latter was a lot more likely option. Bettie didn't want to believe someone would actually attack her, especially being a pregnant woman.

"What can I get you sugar?" the barman asked Sean as he ordered something.

Bettie just smiled. "He didn't call me sugar when I ordered,"

Sean gently kicked Bettie in the leg.

"Where's Phryne?" Graham asked. "And why are we here?"

Bettie was about to take a sip of her drink but

she focused on Ivy as she walked onto the stage smiling.

"I'm here because I want to vote in favour of this new law. You're here to protect me and deal with any idiots that show up," Bettie said.

Graham nodded. "What is this new legislation anyway?"

Bettie waved at Ivy and gave her a thumbs up.

"Basically, if you aren't part of the Federation then you cannot be a Private Eye. The same way psychologists can't be psychologists unless they're a member of the British Psychological Society and the Health and Social Care Council,"

Graham shrugged. "But you aren't doing a job that can kill people,"

Bettie smiled. That was a fair point. A bad point, but a fair one.

"Agreed," Bettie said, "but cops still have to go through training, pass their exams and be authorised by the government in a way. We are simply making sure our people follow a similar standard, we're already seen idiots pretend to be Private Eyes and break laws because they thought that was what Private Eyes did,"

Sean smiled as he was given his diet coke in the exact same glass as Bettie. Both Bettie and Sean put their glasses on the bar.

Ivy clapped her hands together.

Bettie couldn't help but feel like something bad was going to happen. Ivy was the most powerful woman in the Federation she would be a perfect target for the poisoner, and if Ivy was gone, then Bettie had no clue what would happen to the Federation.

"Hello loves," Ivy said, "I presume you have all looked at the legal packs David provided you with,"

As Ivy continued, Bettie wanted to listen to her more and more but a large group of women came towards the bar and blocked her view. Bettie and Sean went to reach for their drinks but the large group stopped them.

Bettie rolled her eyes. This was not what she needed. She was really thirsty after today and all the investigating.

"I know 50% of you voted in earlier pets," Ivy said, "so I think we should just get on with it before we move onto the AGM aspect of the evening,"

Ivy clicked her fingers and a group of waiters and waitresses start walking round with ballot papers and pens to give to all the members who hadn't voted yet.

After a few moments, the large group of women left and Sean went for his drink as soon as he can, but Bettie just smiled as he was focused on the barman a little too much. Then Bettie reached for her drink but Graham tapped her on the shoulder.

"Let me try it," Graham said, firmly.

Bettie rolled her eyes and passed him the drink.

Graham drank a good portion of it and shrugged.

"It tastes fine," Graham said.

Bettie laughed. She was right, she hadn't

expected to be poisoned in the slightest, she was perfectly safe here and-

Sean started coughing.

He grabbed his throat.

Choking.

He collapsed to the ground.

CHAPTER 16
6th August 2022
London, England

Graham felt his stomach twist into a crippling knot as he watched Sean with his ghostly white skin, closed eyes and barely breathing body being rushed off to the nearest hospital.

Graham didn't know what to feel in the slightest. He had felt so angry, rageful and hateful, but most of all he just needed someone to pay for attacking his little nephew that he had grown to love so much.

"That was meant for me," Bettie said.

"What?" Graham asked, slowly realising he wasn't the only person in the convention chamber watching Sean being taken away.

"The group of women. They purposefully made sure me and Sean couldn't get to our drinks. Remember you tapped me on the shoulder so I didn't focus on my drink. Then Sean was focusing too much on the barman, he… probably picked up mine,"

Graham just hugged Bettie. And to his utter annoyance the entire group of Private Eyes, wannabes and other guests simply went around the convention chamber like nothing had even happened.

"What if this isn't what we think?" Bettie asked.

Graham cocked his head. He had been thinking the same thing for a few hours.

"Makes sense. I can't understand why people haven't... you don't die," Graham said.

Bettie smiled. "Glad I'm not the one who thinks that. I know Johnny and I don't doubt he would kill other people given the chance, but no one has died yet,"

Graham gently guided Bettie over to a little private area next to the bar where no one was sitting.

"You don't think the far-right are behind this," Graham said.

Bettie shook her head. "Johnny definitely leaked the sex tape that destroy Phryne's career. He is definitely an awful man that should suffer, but no I don't believe he's the poisoner,"

Graham clicked his fingers. "Poison does tend to be a women's choice of weapon,"

Graham wasn't sure if Bettie was going to argue with that, but she slowly nodded.

"And I think Johnny's more of fire and brimstone type of guy anyway,"

"Graham! Bettie!" Zoey shouted as she rushed over to them wearing her long white lab coat.

"What's up?" Graham asked.

Zoey sounded completely out of breath. "I was working alone in my lab. I tested Sean's coke glass for poison and I found something fascinating,"

Graham and Bettie just looked at each other and gestured Zoey to continue.

"Sean was just poisoned. The poisoner didn't care about duo or tri-poisons, and this time the dosage was a lot higher. The poisoner wanted to kill this time,"

Graham folded his arms. That wasn't good for their current theory about the poisoner not really wanting to kill anyone.

Bettie touched Zoey's arm. "The last two poisoning. What was the dose like? Lethal? Just enough to get sick? Something else?"

"Just enough to get sick," Zoey said.

"What you thinking?" Graham asked.

"I think someone is trying to fame Johnny and the far-right for these attacks, and maybe get them kicked out of the Federation," Bettie said.

It made sense, and if Graham was going to do some poisoning and trying not to kill people, that was probably the plan he would try. But it wasn't exactly without risk.

"What happened to Phryne?" Zoey asked.

Graham shrugged. "I saw her go with the paramedics with Sean,"

Bettie gasped. She knew what had happened.

"Exactly Bet," Zoey said, "I think you're looking for someone else who experienced what Phryne did,"

"And someone who knows about the Federation Conventions," Graham said.

A group of people started to stomp their feet on the main stage. Graham looked at the stage to see Ivy standing to one side with her arms crossed and in the middle, there was Johnny Gray and five other brutish looking men stomping their feet.

"With the current situation going on caused by our women oppressors," Johnny said, "by the power invested in me by all one thousand members of my group, I hereby call for an immediate election for a new President,"

Graham coughed. That was just under half of the entire Federation and yet they all supported this far-right, sexist pig. This wasn't right in the slightest.

"You cannot do that," Graham shouted.

"Shut up Women Enforcer. I don't have to listen to you, supporting the Woman Oppressors," Johnny said.

Bettie pushed on Graham's arm. "Relax. We need to find out who did all this, and we need to buy Ivy time. She knows the Federation rules and regulations better than anyone. She just needs time to find the right one to stop this,"

Graham nodded and went onto the stage.

"Everyone. I am Detective Graham Adams and I have complete jurisdiction over this venue. And I must advise you all to go back to your rooms for the rest of the night, and by morning me and my partner Bettie English would have solved the case,"

Everyone in the convention chamber slowly nodded, looked at each other and started to leave the main stage area.

Johnny grabbed him. "You idiot! You have just-"

Graham shot him a warning look. "Don't you forget I am the police officer. And I could argue you have just assaulted an officer of the law,"

Johnny released him. "You're a traitor to men,"

Then Johnny and his five stupid friends just left.

Graham waved over Bettie, Ivy and Zoey.

"We don't have long," Graham said. "Zoey, I need you to research any cure for the three poisons that we can send to the hospital to help our people,"

Zoey nodded and ran off.

"Ivy," Graham said, "I need you to get me and Bettie security footage from the bar area. We need to see who those women were,"

Ivy nodded and hopped away.

"And me, my love," Bettie said seductively.

Graham smiled. "We need to see who in the Federation had their life destroyed by Johnny Gray,"

And Graham was really looking forward to that.

CHAPTER 17
6th August 2022
London, England

Bettie was flat out furious at this pathetic poisoner. How dare they attack her nephew and try to harm her and her babies. She was going to fucking end the bastard, even if it was the last thing she ever did.

"Here," Graham said, sitting on a very large computer chair as both Bettie and him were in the convention's security headquarters.

There were so many computers buzzing, humming and vibrating that it was hard to focus, but Bettie focused on Graham's computer screen.

The screen showed a group of five women walking towards the bar and Bettie and Sean's drinks couldn't be retrieved by them.

"You look…" Graham said.

Bettie hit him on the back of the head. She honestly did look twenty pounds heavier on the security camera.

"There," Bettie said, pointing to a blond woman.

Bettie and Graham both gasped as they watched the blond woman subtly sprinkle a white powder into Bettie's drink. Then Graham speed it up a little and just as Bettie feared, Sean hadn't been concentrating (well not the drink anyway) and he had picked up hers instead.

Then he collapsed a few moments later.

"Can we see the blond woman's face?" Bettie asked.

Graham typed on the computer a few times, and showed the woman's face perfectly.

Bettie didn't like her small blond face, perfect skin and seductive smile that would probably make any man instantly fall under her spell.

"From what I remember," Bettie said, "the Federation has Facial Recognition of its members,"

Graham nodded and started to run the image through the membership database.

"Whilst that runs," Bettie said, "go onto my Federation Portal and access archived Complaints,"

Graham went onto the Federation's website, typed in Bettie's information and ran a search for anything to do with Johnny Gray.

Ten searches pinned immediately.

"That's strange," Bettie said.

"What?" Graham asked.

"Things never turn up that quick unless someone has recently looked these up in the database,"

"Who has access to 'em?" Graham asked.

Bettie wasn't exactly sure. In a way all members had access to this sort of information in case one of their own cases involved a fellow Private Eye. But considering one of these search results were *classified*, meaning only top-level people had access to them. Bettie wasn't sure.

Bettie focused on the search results themselves.

"We can discount those 3 results because they were about Johnny trying to discredit those men because they were black or gay," Bettie said.

Graham just shook his head. Bettie understood why, Johnny was a complete idiot and he really had poisoned the Federation for too long.

"Discount those four results because it turned out those complaints against Johnny that he faked himself as he was trying to prove women are nothing more than hysterical insane sex objects,"

Graham pointed to the last three. From Bettie could remember about these three complaints and one of them actually led to legal action being taken against Johnny. They were nothing special.

They were simply sexual harassment cases that David settled.

Bettie still wasn't sure how she felt about all this. She was starting to feel like David wasn't a great leader after all, and there was a good chance he cared more about unity than defending the members.

"What happened to the members themselves?" Graham asked. "You know the people Johnny sexually harassed,"

Bettie clicked her fingers. "They all left the Federation and, um, whenever a Private Eye leaves on the resignation form we can write why we left. No one tends to. These three women did,"

Graham stood up.

"All three women claimed David failed them and cared more about protecting the far-right than protecting them,"

"So those three women all have motive for punishing David, blaming the far-right and..." Graham said before he stopped.

"What?" Bettie asked.

"Why attack Joanna?"

Bettie sat down on the computer chair and clicked on the three sexual harassment cases, and to Bettie's utter surprise one of them referenced Joanna.

"Apparently," Bettie said, "Joanna was a witness to the sexually inappropriate behaviour. She made a statement, Johnny threatened too... I'm not saying that out loud and Joanna changed her statement,"

"Is it possible the poisoner believes Joanna's at fault here for her case falling apart?" Graham asked.

Bettie nodded. Bettie's phone buzzed. She looked at it.

"This is from Ivy again. I asked her to look through the ID registration for the convention to see if anyone was using a fake name to get access,"

"And?" Graham asked.

Bettie clicked on the name of the woman who

filed the report where Joanna was a witness. The woman was called Victoria Dawson, and she was a blond woman with perfect skin and she had used a fake name to get access to the convention.

"We have our woman," Bettie said.

Graham nodded.

Bettie and Graham hurried out of the security room.

They had to find Victoria.

Before she could poison anyone else.

CHAPTER 18
6ᵗʰ August 2022
London, England

Graham slowly opened the posh white door to Johnny's hotel room and felt his rage building up. He utterly hated Johnny. He was the worse human ever created and one of the biggest things he hated about this case, was Graham couldn't do anything to Johnny.

For now.

"Don't see him," Bettie said, quietly.

Graham nodded as the two of them went into Johnny's very posh hotel room with fine silk pillows on the sofa, a fully stocked bar and so much more nonsense that this foul idiot didn't deserve.

Graham stopped. He heard some moaning or something coming from the bedroom. Graham pointed towards it to Bettie.

They slowly went over the hard oak floors towards the bedroom.

When Graham reached the wide open door, he couldn't help but smile as he saw a completely paralyzed Johnny Gray completely naked and a very tall (and fully clothed) blond woman standing next to him with a knife.

Graham had to admire how Victoria had tied Johnny to the bed and made his body completely limp.

"Hello Victoria," Bettie said.

Victoria simply turned around and smiled at the two of them like they were too good friends she had known forever. Graham hadn't been expecting that.

"You know we can't let you kill him," Graham said.

He actually hated saying that. Until then Graham hadn't realised how much he absolutely hated Johnny.

"Why not?" Victoria asked. "He harassed me for months and when I said no more look at all this. I was forced out of the Federation, no one wanted to hire me as a Private Eye any more, my life ended,"

Bettie took a few steps forward. "I am sorry,"

Victoria shook her head. "This isn't about you. Bettie you were great. I saw your talk yesterday. If I had known you back then maybe things would have been different,"

Bettie nodded. Graham knew it wasn't an act, he knew that Bettie would have honestly tried to protect her better.

"But I didn't. And now my life is over. Now his life needs to be over," Victoria said raising the knife.

Graham took a few steps forward.

Victoria held the blade to Johnny's throat.

"I will kill him," she said coldly.

"We don't doubt that for a second," Graham said, "but I want to know why first. What was the plan with all of this? And why target Bettie?"

Victoria swallowed hard when she saw the baby bump up close.

Her hands turned shaky.

"Oh god. Oh god. Oh god!" Victoria said.

Bettie started to walk closer.

"Stay back!" Victoria shouted.

Graham looked at Bettie. He didn't want her here. And he had to sadly save Johnny.

"What was the plan?" Graham asked.

"David was an idiot. He allowed Johnny to get away with all this!" Victoria shouted. "He is one of them!"

Bettie gasped, and Graham had come to the same realisation. Maybe David really wasn't the man he claimed to be.

"Joanna! She... she could have helped me. She didn't!"

Bettie waved her hands about and came closer.

"She was threatened. She was scared," Bettie said.

"How the fuck did you think I felt!" Victoria shouted.

"Why me?" Bettie asked. Bettie placed her hands on her baby bump. "Why us?"

Tears filled Victoria's eyes. She fell to the floor. Putting her face in her knees.

"I'm so sorry. I'm… so sorry," Victoria said.

Johnny laughed. He shot up. Grabbing the knife.

"No!" Graham shouted.

Johnny pressed the knife against Victoria's throat.

"Fucking woman slut!" Johnny shouted.

Graham flew at him.

Jump on him.

Graham whacked him across the face.

Bettie grabbed the knife.

"Idiot!" Johnny shouted. "Now that slut will-"

Graham punched his lights out.

Clearly Victoria wasn't as good at paralysing poisons as she hoped.

The sounds of Victoria's crying echoed around the hotel room and Graham just didn't feel good about any of this.

The far-right man who started all of this got away free. A victim of sexual harassment and who's life was destroyed by him was going to prison. And the Federation wasn't going to change so everything could repeat itself.

Graham just looked at Bettie who was hugging Victoria and allowing her hands to feel the baby bump.

"I'm so sorry," Victoria said.

Bettie simply held her. "I know… I know you are,"

Then Bettie smiled at Graham, and there was something in that smile that gave him hope.

Not hope for Victoria. She was going to prison no matter what.

But hope that history couldn't repeat itself.

And something very grand was about to happen.

CHAPTER 19
7th August 2022
London, England

Graham was really pleased when Zoey had phoned in the middle of the night and revealed how she had successfully had cures to all three poisons, and the brilliant hospital staff were delivering them as she spoke.

Even after a full day of clearing up Victoria's mess, filling in the paperwork on the case and watching Bettie talk on a few more excellent panels, he was still really pleased to know that everyone was okay. Especially Sean.

At the closing ceremony, Phryne, Sean and Bettie sat around a small wooden table as Graham walked over with their non-poisoned drinks in the convention chamber in front of the main stage.

Graham was still impressed to see so many people happily sitting and standing as they waited for David to close the convention officially and announce who was going to be the next President.

Everyone was talking, muttering and moaning amongst themselves as they wondered who it was going to be. Some people believed it would be Joanna, others believed it would be Johnny and others just didn't know.

Graham really hoped it wasn't any of them. From what he had seen in the past few weeks, there wasn't anyone capable of being the new President, well Bettie was more than capable but no one would sadly want her.

Especially as she had said to Graham last night that being President was more about covering the Federation's backside than helping people. Graham had completely agreed, he hated it. Bettie had showed him how wonderful and amazing the Federation could be, but it just had to have the right leader.

And the right leader was never going to come sadly.

Graham loved the wonderful scents of lavender, oranges and cedarwood that filled the entire convention chamber and it left a strange taste of seawater like he experienced going on holiday as a child. There was always plenty of cedarwood and oranges and cloves there.

Graham put everyone's drinks down and he laughed when Sean frowned at Phryne's diet cola. Graham had a feeling Sean and Bettie were going to be avoiding it for a long, long time to come.

Out of the corner of Graham's eyes two

uniformed officers bought in a handcuffed Victoria and sat down at the very back of the audience. Some people muttered but Graham didn't care.

He still didn't entirely understand why Bettie had insisted (and forced) him to have Victoria present for this bit, but it was something about making everything right.

Graham didn't know how she would make everything right, considering everything that had happened, but he really hoped for everyone's sake that she could manage to find a way.

"Hello everyone," David said.

Graham had to admit it was great seeing David so fit and healthy and looking great after what happened. He was wearing a tailored made black suit, red tie and he seemed so happy to be alive.

Bettie, Sean and Phryne were frowning. Graham wasn't sure why.

"I would like to give a massive congratulations and thank you to the amazing two people that solved this case," David said. "Now a round of applause for Bettie English and Graham Adams,"

Everyone clapped.

Bettie smiled and stood up. "Thank you David, but I would like to say something if you may,"

David didn't look too sure but he gestured Bettie should join him on the stage. Bettie waved at Graham to follow and he did.

Once on the stage, Bettie shook her head at David.

"Thank you, and I am glad to see our fearless leader alive and well," Graham said, "And I am very pleased to see the law change David proposed was approved, so I am sure the new President can make the UK Government make that law. But there is a problem,"

Everyone looked confused at Bettie.

Bettie just looked at David.

"David Osborne, I hereby declare you a traitor to the Federation," Bettie said.

Everyone muttered something negative.

"For too long," Bettie said, "you have lied and manipulated and abused your power within the Federation. You pretend to Protect the membership and you try to keep everyone united. But that is a lie,"

Johnny and his friends stood up. Graham shot them a warning look.

"You manipulated all of us thinking you were only doing what was in the best interest of the Federation. You kept lying to us saying that the far-left, far-right and everyone else was needed. But you were only ever interested in keeping your far-right friends close,"

Graham noticed David's happiness started to fade.

"And David Osborne," Bettie said, "I can now guess that you were not looking up the Republic of Private Eyes, Johnny Gray and the other two names on Thursday night out of concern. You were looking to officially form the Republic to house your far-right friends safely and you probably want to make Johnny Gray the new President,"

David was deadly silent. Graham was horrified at all this.

"I'll give it to you," Bettie said, "you probably imagined your secrets would die with Victoria Dawson. But I will reveal to everyone the simple truth. When three women came to you and filed sexual harassment reports against Johnny Gray, you bent the rules, manipulated people and make sure it was the victims that left the Federation and not your friends,"

Johnny and his friends walked towards the stage. Graham firmly stood in their way. They weren't getting close to Bettie.

"There was a lot more things I would like to say to you David Osborne, but there is one thing that will make my point very clear," Bettie said.

"What is that?" David slowly said.

"To paraphrase the words that started the downfall of UK Prime Minister chamberlain. You have sat in that chair for too long for the amount of good you have done. So by god go!"

Everyone fell silent.

David looked like he was about to say something, but Graham pointed a finger at him.

Ivy walked on stage. "And what you just said Miss English 'So by God go!' Phryne helped me understand that would reach the legal criteria for a certain rule in the Private Eye Act. Meaning David would not be able to choose his successor,"

Johnny frowned and turned to face everyone.

"Men! We must be strong against these women. These women will keep trying to steal our freedoms from us! We must take a stand now!" Johnny shouted.

But no one was listening. No one cared. That made Graham really happy.

Ivy looked at David. "My final act as Secretary General of the Federation is this,"

A tear dripped down Ivy's face and he didn't know how painful this must be for her. Finding out one of your old friends was basically a monster.

Then Graham smiled when Bettie placed a gentle hand on Ivy's.

Bettie just looked at David. "David Osborne under Section 50 of the Private Eye Act, I hereby declare you have broken the Federation Code on accounts of Manipulation, Abuse and Lying. There is no greater wrong for you and there is no punishment short of death that would even start to make what you did right,"

David gulped.

"Therefore," Bettie said, "I remove you from office immediately and call upon our members to elect a new leader,"

David sank to his knees. Graham smiled as he watched all the happiness, life and arrogance drain from his face. Graham was glad David was suffering just like those three women had.

Bettie looked at the audience. "Who shall be

elected to be leader?"

To Graham's utter shock, everyone was silent but they quickly looked at each other, nodded and pointed to Bettie.

They actually wanted Bettie to be the new President.

Graham couldn't deny how cute Bettie looked as she was utterly shocked, confused and not sure she really wanted this.

Ivy held Bettie's hands and Graham could barely hear what they were saying.

"They have democratically elected you, Miss Bettie English to be the new President. Do you accept this honour?" Ivy asked.

Bettie looked at Graham. Graham just blew her a massive kiss and smiled. Whatever she choose he would love, support and treasure her forever.

Bettie nodded. She was now President of the Federation, but she gave such an evil smile to Johnny and his friends.

"Johnny Gray," Bettie said angrily. "Unlike David I will not focus on unity. I will focus on what is right. So I hereby strip you, your friends and any far-right person of their license and membership to the Federation. And because of the new law, you will never be a Private Eye again, and you will suffer for what you did to all your victims,"

Johnny dived forward. Graham grabbed him.

Three security guards stepped forward and escorted Johnny and his friends out of the convention.

Then Graham went up and hugged Bettie hard. She had done the impossible, and he damn well loved her for it.

Bettie and Graham just looked at Victoria as she sat at the very back in handcuffs and she simply muttered *thank you*.

"The Federation Protects," Bettie muttered.

CHAPTER 20
8th August 2022
Canterbury, England

After some utterly amazing, flat out wonderful after-parties last night, Bettie was so glad to be back in her stunning office in Canterbury just above the breath-taking cobblestone Highstreet.

Bettie really did love the office. Even back as she walked in just the sight of her wooden desk, wonderful sofa and thin glass windows were such a welcoming sight, and it truly meant that the world that returned to normal for her.

Now she was back, there were no more political crazies, conspiracies or poisoners that would and could try to kill her. Bettie opened her window slightly and flat out love the sweet smell of the freshly baked bread that would easily dissolve into buttery deliciousness on her tongue, creamy cakes and all the other sensationally baked good that the local bakeries were cooking up.

And one of Bettie's most favourite sounds, the talking and laughing of university students and the playing of music by the street performers filled the office. And Bettie was so glad to be back.

But now she was back as President.

Even now she was shocked as anything that the Private Eyes wanted her to be in charge. There was a hell of a lot to do and a lot to clear up in the Federation, but Bettie was really excited about it.

Because unlike David, she actually cared about the Private Eyes she was elected to serve. Bettie couldn't care less about politics, upset and everything else that David had, because at the end of the day, if the Federation cared more about unity than justice and morality. Then what was the point of it?

There wasn't one.

Bettie truly believed in the saying *The Federation Protects*. Yet it was only after the past few days, Bettie had realised how far the Federation had moved away from that ideal and that mission.

She wanted to get that ideal back.

As Bettie sat on her little sofa and watched all the amazing university students walk, laugh and joke up and down the cobblestone high street, Bettie really knew how lucky she was.

Sure, there would be problems ahead and she would have made enemies in the Federation by disgracing David. But she didn't care because that was tomorrow's problem.

And at least Bettie knew that her family was okay

now. Phryne had almost lost Sean for a second time, and that had seemed to buck her ideas up so she was now talking to Sean and Harry about moving them back in and probably mending all the broken fences.

Bettie still have the heart to tell Phryne, those fences and bridges and bonds between family hadn't been broken. They had been shattered.

But Bettie knew they could work it all out and put all the damage behind them, and Bettie and Graham would help them as much as they could with the twins coming soon.

So thankfully Bettie's amazing, sometimes dysfunctional family was okay.

Bettie watched an elderly man struggle to walk down the street and thankfully two young women offered to help him, and he accepted. Another simple act of kindness that made Bettie smile.

Bettie was a little surprised when David had said to her as she left that he never wanted her to be President, and she had kind of always known that.

David was probably one of the best lairs Bettie had ever met. So as Graham drove them home Bettie had investigated David a little more, and she was flat out shocked.

It turned out there had been hundreds of women, gay and black people that David had forced out of the Federation over the decades because he probably thought it was easier to kick out the victims than upset the abusers. And possibly cause the Federation to fall away.

Bettie seriously didn't care about that, and with her kicking out the far-right members. The Federation had lost about 40% of its membership, a lot of sponsors and even more money in membership fees.

It still felt good. Because now there were a lot less people who were abusers and haters that wanted to ruin the Federation for the rest of them.

Since that was ultimately the difference between Victoria and Johnny. It had taken Bettie ages to work this all out, but Victoria hadn't wanted people to actually suffer. She had wanted David, Joanna and maybe Bettie to suffer, because some sort of perceived wrong.

But not permanently hurt them.

And it was Victoria that had told the waiter to tell Bettie and Graham she was in Johnny's room. That's how they had found her so quickly.

Johnny was the opposite. He didn't care what lives he ruined, shattered and decimated. For him, it was all about proving his stupid ideas and making himself feel important. Instead of him being the weak pathetic man everyone knew him to be.

Yet the hardest aspect of this case was probably the legal work David had asked Phryne to do, and when Sean asked Bettie about that on the drive home. It had taken her a few minutes to answer, but the answer was a lot clearer.

When she remembered that David was a master manipulator, Bettie understood that he wasn't concerned about theft of funds and Articles and what

Bettie had originally believed to be about government blackmail.

A little research revealed David had been stealing funds for years and he was trying to find a legal argument to justify it in case he ever got caught. That's why he asked Phryne for help.

But Bettie was really impressed with his plan for the Article 16 and 20, which Bettie guessed David was going to collect when he packed up his office for the final time. Bettie fully believed it was David that was going to steal those Articles and blackmail the UK government in case the country even moved too far to the left for his liking.

Which was probably always the case.

And when Bettie considered how rarely people checked to see if the Articles were still in the safe where they were kept, Bettie reckoned David could have blackmailed the government for years before anyone at the Federation noticed.

So as Bettie opened her laptop for a very nice relaxing day before she started her first official day as President tomorrow, Bettie was really looking forward to the future.

She didn't know what the future was going to bring, but she knew it would be fun, filled with laughs and plenty of amazing cases to solve.

And to Bettie that was very much a perfect life.

GET YOUR FREE AND EXCLUSIVE SHORT STORY NOW! LEARN ABOUT NEMESIO'S PAST!

https://www.subscribepage.com/fireheart

Keep up to date with exclusive deals on Connor Whiteley's Books, as well as the latest news about new releases and so much more!

Sign up for the Grab a Book and Chill Monthly newsletter, and you'll get one **FREE** ebook just for signing up: Agents of The Emperor Collection.

Sign Up Now!

https://dl.bookfunnel.com/f4p5xkprbk

About the author:

Connor Whiteley is the author of over 60 books in the sci-fi fantasy, nonfiction psychology and books for writer's genre and he is a Human Branding Speaker and Consultant.

He is a passionate warhammer 40,000 reader, psychology student and author.

Who narrates his own audiobooks and he hosts The Psychology World Podcast.

All whilst studying Psychology at the University of Kent, England.

Also, he was a former Explorer Scout where he gave a speech to the Maltese President in August 2018 and he attended Prince Charles' 70th Birthday Party at Buckingham Palace in May 2018.

Plus, he is a self-confessed coffee lover!

OTHER SHORT STORIES BY CONNOR WHITELEY

<u>Mystery Short Stories:</u>
Poison In The Candy Cane
Christmas Innocence
You Better Watch Out
Christmas Theft
Trouble In Christmas
Smell of The Lake
Problem In A Car
Theft, Past and Team
Embezzler In The Room
A Strange Way To Go
A Horrible Way To Go
Ann Awful Way To Go
An Old Way To Go
A Fishy Way To Go
A Pointy Way To Go
A High Way To Go
A Fiery Way To Go
A Glassy Way To Go
A Chocolatey Way To Go
Kendra Detective Mystery Collection Volume 1
Kendra Detective Mystery Collection Volume 2
Stealing A Chance At Freedom

Glassblowing and Death
Theft of Independence
Cookie Thief
Marble Thief
Book Thief
Art Thief
Mated At The Morgue
The Big Five Whoopee Moments
Stealing An Election
Mystery Short Story Collection Volume 1
Mystery Short Story Collection Volume 2

Science Fiction Short Stories:
The First Rememberer
Life of A Rememberer
System of Wonder
Lifesaver
Remarkable Way She Died
The Interrogation of Annabella Stormic
Blade of The Emperor
Arbiter's Truth
Computation of Battle
Old One's Wrath
Puppets and Masters
Ship of Plague
Interrogation
Edge of Failure

One Way Choice
Acceptable Losses
Balance of Power
Good Idea At The Time
Escape Plan
Escape In The Hesitation
Inspiration In Need
Singing Warriors
Knowledge is Power
Killer of Polluters
Climate of Death
The Family Mailing Affair
Defining Criminality
The Martian Affair
A Cheating Affair
The Little Café Affair
Mountain of Death
Prisoner's Fight
Claws of Death
Bitter Air
Honey Hunt
Blade On A Train

<u>Fantasy Short Stories:</u>
City of Snow
City of Light
City of Vengeance

Dragons, Goats and Kingdom
Smog The Pathetic Dragon
Don't Go In The Shed
The Tomato Saver
The Remarkable Way She Died
The Bloodied Rose
Asmodia's Wrath
Heart of A Killer
Emissary of Blood
Dragon Coins
Dragon Tea
Dragon Rider
Sacrifice of the Soul
Heart of The Flesheater
Heart of The Regent
Heart of The Standing
Feline of The Lost
Heart of The Story
City of Fire
Awaiting Death

Other books by Connor Whiteley:
Bettie English Private Eye Series
A Very Private Woman
The Russian Case
A Very Urgent Matter
A Case Most Personal
Trains, Scots and Private Eyes
The Federation Protects

The Fireheart Fantasy Series
Heart of Fire
Heart of Lies
Heart of Prophecy
Heart of Bones
Heart of Fate

City of Assassins (Urban Fantasy)
City of Death
City of Marytrs
City of Pleasure
City of Power

Agents of The Emperor
Return of The Ancient Ones
Vigilance
Angels of Fire
Kingmaker

The Garro Series- Fantasy/Sci-fi
GARRO: GALAXY'S END
GARRO: RISE OF THE ORDER
GARRO: END TIMES
GARRO: SHORT STORIES
GARRO: COLLECTION
GARRO: HERESY
GARRO: FAITHLESS
GARRO: DESTROYER OF WORLDS
GARRO: COLLECTIONS BOOK 4-6
GARRO: MISTRESS OF BLOOD
GARRO: BEACON OF HOPE
GARRO: END OF DAYS

Winter Series- Fantasy Trilogy Books
WINTER'S COMING
WINTER'S HUNT
WINTER'S REVENGE
WINTER'S DISSENSION

Miscellaneous:
RETURN
FREEDOM
SALVATION
Reflection of Mount Flame
The Masked One
The Great Deer

All books in 'An Introductory Series':
BIOLOGICAL PSYCHOLOGY 3RD EDITION
COGNITIVE PSYCHOLOGY THIRD EDITION
SOCIAL PSYCHOLOGY- 3RD EDITION
ABNORMAL PSYCHOLOGY 3RD EDITION
PSYCHOLOGY OF RELATIONSHIPS- 3RD EDITION
DEVELOPMENTAL PSYCHOLOGY 3RD EDITION
HEALTH PSYCHOLOGY
RESEARCH IN PSYCHOLOGY
A GUIDE TO MENTAL HEALTH AND TREATMENT AROUND THE WORLD- A GLOBAL LOOK AT DEPRESSION
FORENSIC PSYCHOLOGY
THE FORENSIC PSYCHOLOGY OF THEFT, BURGLARY AND OTHER CRIMES AGAINST PROPERTY
CRIMINAL PROFILING: A FORENSIC PSYCHOLOGY GUIDE TO FBI PROFILING AND GEOGRAPHICAL AND STATISTICAL PROFILING.
CLINICAL PSYCHOLOGY
FORMULATION IN PSYCHOTHERAPY

PERSONALITY PSYCHOLOGY AND
INDIVIDUAL DIFFERENCES
CLINICAL PSYCHOLOGY
REFLECTIONS VOLUME 1
CLINICAL PSYCHOLOGY
REFLECTIONS VOLUME 2
CULT PSYCHOLOGY
Police Psychology

A Psychology Student's Guide To University
How Does University Work?
A Student's Guide To University And Learning
University Mental Health and Mindset

Companion guides:
BIOLOGICAL PSYCHOLOGY 2ND EDITION WORKBOOK
COGNITIVE PSYCHOLOGY 2ND EDITION WORKBOOK
SOCIOCULTURAL PSYCHOLOGY 2ND EDITION WORKBOOK
ABNORMAL PSYCHOLOGY 2ND EDITION WORKBOOK
PSYCHOLOGY OF HUMAN RELATIONSHIPS 2ND EDITION WORKBOOK

HEALTH PSYCHOLOGY WORKBOOK
FORENSIC PSYCHOLOGY WORKBOOK

Audiobooks by Connor Whiteley:
BIOLOGICAL PSYCHOLOGY
COGNITIVE PSYCHOLOGY
SOCIOCULTURAL PSYCHOLOGY
ABNORMAL PSYCHOLOGY
PSYCHOLOGY OF HUMAN RELATIONSHIPS
HEALTH PSYCHOLOGY
DEVELOPMENTAL PSYCHOLOGY
RESEARCH IN PSYCHOLOGY
FORENSIC PSYCHOLOGY
GARRO: GALAXY'S END
GARRO: RISE OF THE ORDER
GARRO: SHORT STORIES
GARRO: END TIMES
GARRO: COLLECTION
GARRO: HERESY
GARRO: FAITHLESS
GARRO: DESTROYER OF WORLDS
GARRO: COLLECTION BOOKS 4-6
GARRO: COLLECTION BOOKS 1-6

Business books:
[TIME MANAGEMENT: A GUIDE FOR STUDENTS AND WORKERS](#)
[LEADERSHIP: WHAT MAKES A GOOD LEADER? A GUIDE FOR STUDENTS AND WORKERS.](#)
[BUSINESS SKILLS: HOW TO SURVIVE THE BUSINESS WORLD? A GUIDE FOR STUDENTS, EMPLOYEES AND EMPLOYERS.](#)
[BUSINESS COLLECTION](#)

GET YOUR FREE BOOK AT:
WWW.CONNORWHITELEY.NET

www.ingramcontent.com/pod-product-compliance
Lightning Source LLC
LaVergne TN
LVHW011836060526
838200LV00053B/4059